MW00424404

Adjunct

Geoff Cebula

ISBN: 9781521387412

To Emily

One final tip, when adjuncting on an overloaded schedule, is to always be working. That winter semester was my harvest time, my time for 12-14 hour days, for working weekends and for squeezing every last amount of work out of each day that I could. […] And keep in mind that summer, with its lull in classes, will eventually come.

- Advice from "Piss Poor Prof" published by *Inside Higher Ed*

The mouse wasn't going in the wrong direction so much as it was walking cat food the entire time.

- Rebecca Schuman writing for *Slate*

Part One: Wednesday

CHAPTER ONE

Elena always came to departmental meetings, even after they stopped inviting her. Like any dedicated faculty member, she was eager to show her interest in planning the future of the Modern Language Department and cultivating a friendly and productive culture among its members.

It didn't matter that attendance at these meetings was no longer listed among the responsibilities delineated in her contract now that she was an adjunct. Her investment in this Department remained as great as ever, and it was important for her to show it. After all, Sveta never used to come to the meetings, and now Bellwether College no longer taught Russian. No one had ever explicitly suggested that these two facts were related to each other, but Derek had referenced Sveta's absence at the meetings in a knowing tone after the decision to discontinue Russian had been made—and whatever one thought of Derek, he seemed to understand a fair bit about how the Department worked. So Elena made a point of continuing to attend these meetings. Indeed, she usually made a point of arriving early in order to make a little small talk with the other faculty and to secure a seat right in the front row.

Today, however, was turning into a disaster. And it was all because of goddamn Pietro and his corporate fascist claptrap. Forgetting that she needed to go to campus today, Elena had scheduled a 10am call with Pietro, her biggest freelancing client, to discuss her last round of copyedits for his book *Musso-Lean-in: Management Advice from the Great Dictators*. Usually, if she had to talk to a client before work she would make the call from a coffee shop near campus, but she was up late the previous night finishing a recommendation letter for a student who had never spoken during her

1

Italian film class but evidently found it "an invaluable facet [sic] of her educational experience," and also she only remembered that the meeting was today after her oatmeal was already on the stove. Moreover, she couldn't reschedule with Pietro because one of the main reasons for this conversation was to determine when he would send her a check for her work over the past two months.

Of course, Pietro didn't sign on to talk until 10:17 and the conversation lasted longer than planned, nearly half-an-hour, at the end of which—after an interminable series of digressions about the hottest spots for EDM in Rome—Pietro finally admitted that he had not yet read the latest copy, but promised to put the check in the mail as soon as he did. Thus, Elena finally embarked on the twenty-five minute drive to Bellwether at 10:45—giving herself much less cushion than she would have planned under normal circumstances—only to find that Prospect Pike, the faithful artery that always brought her to work, had been fatally clogged by a lightening-stricken tree. Blaring NPR to calm herself down, she watched the clock tick steadily onward, as her car slowly edged along the detour route, making it all the way to 11:17 before she finally pulled through the campus gate.

Thankfully, the main faculty parking lot was right outside David L. Howlsley Hall, where the meeting was schedule. If everything went smoothly from here on out, Elena could still make it on time. Usually, the lot didn't fill until the afternoon, so she should be able to find a space on the second level pretty easily, and then at a brisk walk she could make it to Howlsley just on time (assuming she didn't slip on the ice in between—she had slipped on the ice before and doing it now would easily eat up a whole minute). There wouldn't be much time for small talk with the other faculty, but she didn't really want to do that anyway. And the main thing was simply to be there on time. Punctuality would help show her seriousness, reliability, dedication, and eagerness to participate in shaping the department. It would also add another little piece to the image of indispensability that she was working hard to establish. If faculty meetings never started without her, she fantasized, it was just a small step to starting to think that they *couldn't* start without her. Maintaining this impression meant that she needed to park and sprint to the Department within the next eleven minutes—again, a doable task if she minded the ice.

But then, as she pulled up to the security gate, she felt a sudden terror that maybe she had forgotten her ID card. Indeed, she felt a sinking certainty that she must have forgotten it and this fatal error would make her late for the meeting; maybe she would even miss it entirely, and her car would circle the campus aimlessly for hours until it ran out of gas. As her fingernail flipped through the cards in her wallet, she saw her brief career flash before her eyes: the passive-aggressive exchanges with senior faculty, her constant fear at facing an expectant classroom, the endless cloud of chalk dust… The radio news was airing a special report on New Orleans jazz funerals, and she imagined herself lying in a coffin, discarded in an alley just off the parade route, forgotten in death because she had failed to assert her existence in life… She felt unexpectedly sanguine at the prospect of it all coming to end here. Maybe this was always what had to happen. Maybe today was really a new—at that moment she noticed the ID card sitting in her cup holder, where she had put it just twenty minutes before, when stopped in malicious traffic, in order to save time when she finally reached campus. With a silent prayer of thanks to the universe for not being excessively malevolent, she drove into the parking garage.

It was only after she passed the second completely-packed level that she started to sense something was amiss. Why were there so many cars on campus? Unless… The sense of fatalism returned as Elena suddenly remembered that it was actually *Wednesday* morning, the busiest scheduling block for classes. She had forgotten because the Department usually held faculty meetings on less-busy Thursday mornings to avoid scheduling conflicts, but they had moved this one due to an info session for the Study in Berlin! program, which meant parking in the main lot was far from assured.

Elena slowed down momentarily before driving up to the top level. She was frozen by indecision over whether it was better to keep searching here or to turn around and drive to the next lot. Just as she decided to keep going, a red sedan suddenly accelerated and swerved around her, cutting so close to Elena's front bumper that she had to slam on the brakes. Slightly delirious from anger, Elena watched the driver pull into an open space far up ahead in the next row. It took only a quick spin around the last several spaces to confirm that this was, in fact, the last open space in the garage. Not only that, but the driver who emerged from the sedan was Amrita, who taught Hindi and Urdu in the Department and, Elena always suspected, was a main reason for her own hours being reduced. After all, the introductory classes for Italian and Hindi/Urdu were both struggling for enrollments, and neither could boast a substantial number of majors (though there was now *one* self-designed major in Italian, thanks to Elena's hard work). She had never actually witnessed Amrita speaking to Victor about the "future of the Italian program," but she had felt a certain static when passing either of them in the hall last year. Admittedly, she was on edge all last year and had started searching every interaction for clues about whether Bellwether would renew her contract, and it was just possible that she was simply reading too much into things. But even as she told herself that she was probably just being paranoid, part of her felt certain that the other faculty members representing the "lesser taught languages" (i.e., those that weren't Spanish) had been conspiring to bump her off, and if anything, Elena should have been working harder to make alliances for a preemptive strike.

Kill or be killed, right? If the College was making cuts anyway, why shouldn't she be doing everything she could to redirect the knife? That's clearly what everyone else was doing…

And now there was Amrita, walking slowly down the center of the aisle, apparently oblivious to the car patiently following behind her. Elena nervously tapped the steering wheel while her car crept toward the exit at the casual pace set by her colleague. She might have called out to Amrita, but for the moment she was content to follow passive aggressively behind, thinking about what would happen if she made just a light little push on the gas pedal… There would most likely be no one else in the garage until several minutes after classes let out at 11:50…Her uncle up in Fallen Hopes could do a little fender work no questions asked… Elena would never do something like that, but one had to admit that Amrita's giant, red faux-leather purse would make a perfect target…

CHAPTER TWO

"Have you ever wondered how many people you would have to murder to get tenure?" Connie had once asked Elena.

It was late in the afternoon. They had been sitting silently in Pterosaur Coffee for a little over an hour. Both were now looking up from their grading, feeling a little dazed from the faded high of sugar and caffeine. Sensing some hesitation, Connie added: "Just so you know, I have thought about it. And I don't think it's weird to just wonder about these things. Just think about it. The U.S. Treasury Secretary must have the number 'five' firmly implanted in his brain; every morning he probably secretly hopes to see the headline, 'Unprecedented String of Tragedies Rocks the White House and Congress'... For me, the number is three, maybe four. One to open a new tenure line, one more to ensure that Tom will become acting chair, and then I'm thinking one or two more in the administration. I know that Bill has been pushing the whole digital thing, so he has to go. There might be additional pressure from higher up—I'm still investigating...But for now, the number is three."

Elena didn't respond immediately, instead looking down at her papers. Connie eyed her skeptically, not quite sure whether her friend just was actually distracted or just taking a theatrical pause, maybe to make it seem like she was thinking about this for the first time.

"I don't think there's a path," Elena admitted finally. "That's how bad things are—there's not even anyone I could kill to get onto the tenure track. Really, it's more likely the Dean of the Humanities would have me executed. That way, they could make a clean break with the Italian program."

This conversation happened almost a year ago. Back then, Elena's position was still labeled as "Italian Coordinator" and officially counted as five-eights of a full-time faculty position. It was a pretty good arrangement for her, overall. The word "coordinator" sounded impressive in her title (even though in reality there was only one other Italian instructor to coordinate), and she enjoyed saying it. More importantly, being at "five-eighths" afforded her at least a moderate degree of financial security. Of course, she could never quite figure out how her various functions in the department added up to just over half-time. It was almost as if the administration had set the number five-eighths more or less independently of any actual estimate of the time required to meet the responsibilities of the position, perhaps regarding the number five-eighths a sacred figure with inherent mystical properties. Whatever their reasoning, Elena was grateful to have this five-eighths because she knew a precipitous drop awaited her below that threshold. Losing the "coordinator" title would mean being hired by the individual class, which meant even less job security than she had now and, of course, significantly lower pay. It would almost certainly mean taking another job, maybe translating or copyediting, to pay the bills. Perhaps one reason why she was a little distracted while talking with Connie was that the administration hadn't responded yet about renewing her contract. There was no timeline for when they would respond, but Elena interpreted every day as an additional red flag.

"Isn't there anyone in your department you'd kill just for fun?" Connie asked just to test out her friend's response. "Like for example, there's this grumpy old Russian guy over at Wanesdale. He always acts a little put upon, as if people see him as old and out of touch, but there's also this weird special-genius aura around him that he clings to. (I think he knew some famous poet or something back in the day, and he's, like, a big deal in their field.) Anyway, he doesn't listen when any of the women in the department speak, and one of our female grad students told me he practically made her take dictation for one of his articles. I heard he used to just laugh off accusations of sexism, but he's more savvy now. He'll sometimes talk about the importance of strong women's voices, and then he'll talk over me at every faculty meeting… Remember that Argento movie where the killer put nails under that singer's eyelids to make her watch his murders? I kinda want to do something similar to him—but he'd have to watch panels with all female speakers.—These thoughts really never occur to you?"

"I do love that movie," Elena smiled slightly. "I guess academia just leads to morbid thoughts…" she added absentmindedly.

"You're right about that!" Connie was either very enthusiastic about this topic or very reluctant to get back to grading. "When I was a finalist for Michigan last year, one of the grad students told me the names of the other candidates. So I started stalking them on social media to see if they would post anything like, 'So happy to be joining the faculty of Harvard next year,' or 'God, I just fucked up my campus visit at Michigan. Now digging a hole to live in.' And all that's, like, normal, right?" (No pause for a response.)

6

"But then, I kinda got to a dark place. I was looking up all the flights from their home cities to Ann Arbor and the weather conditions and wondering about the likelihood of a plane crash. I mean, obviously a plane crash would be very sad. A lot of innocent people would also die. But they do happen sometimes, so why couldn't it just happen to be this one, you know? And of course, there were also the road conditions. More people die in car accidents than from air travel. And the roads get icy up there around February. So then, I was also asking myself how they would go about completing the search if the committee chair also died while picking the candidate up from the airport. And my thoughts kinda just kept going from there." Connie paused for a moment. "You know, they sent physical letters of rejection in the mail. They came in April, and no one updated the wiki, so, like, I figured out I didn't get the job sooner, but I was thinking about all of this for a long time. Does thinking about this make me a bad person? You'd tell me if I was a bad person, right?"

Elena did what she normally did when asked this question—she shrugged. When Connie didn't seem satisfied with this response, Elena added: "At least you're no longer a grad student."

"Yeah, I have that." Connie looked down at the splash of enamel-colored liquid she had nursed in her coffee cup for the past half hour. This wasn't exactly the first time someone had deflected the question of whether she was a bad person. But to be fair, Elena had seen her at her worst: general exams, dissertating, dating Erica, applying for jobs, getting back together with Erica, applying to more jobs, getting over Erica... (Hm. There were a lot of bad years in there...) And it was fun to complain about grad students while the feeling of no longer being one was still fresh, so Connie cheered up a little bit. "One of the first-years in our department was complaining about the stipend. I was like, just stop talking, I'd kill to still be paid for taking classes."

"I feel like the bar keeps lowering for what would make you kill someone."

It was a fair point. "Does that worry you?"

"No," Elena said slowly. "I don't think you would actually kill anyone. A real murderer would keep quiet about her intentions."

"So, maybe I'm the one who should be worried..."

Elena started in again on grading her tests and quickly gave up. Teddy Soplica had either entirely neglected her request to be more careful with his handwriting or decided to stop writing in traditional Latin characters in favor of a new pictographic language of his own invention. It would be another long night trying to figure out how to grade these.

"Now, why would I want to kill anyone?"

CHAPTER THREE

Departmental meetings were always conducted by the Chair. In previous years, the format had ranged from casual discussion among the faculty to baroquely detailed presentations. Now that Victor was in charge, the meeting essentially consisted of a dispassionate reading from the main points of a slideshow presentation thrown together haphazardly while watching Rachel Maddow the night before.

Today's presentation outlined the central findings of a report issued by the Moahil Loch consulting firm, which had been hired by the College to address its current budget crisis. Unsurprisingly, the firm had determined the Modern Language Department to be one of the main weak points in the College's moral and financial constitution: by offering courses across too great a range of national cultures, the Department was a main offender in what the firm called "identity dissonance," i.e., the cultivation of interests that for the vast majority of students wouldn't carry over into their professional identities later in life. Such "dissonance" was essentially harmful to students, the report elaborated, as longitudinal studies had shown the potential for a decrease in long-term earnings among those students who delayed too long in choosing a marketable major. Moreover, these superfluous and essentially deleterious classes were contributing to budget shortfalls and therefore effectively diverting funds from programs, like the schools of business and engineering, that did actually satisfy the College's main objective of producing well-trained professionals for the local economy.

It was now incumbent upon Victor to communicate this message to the very parasites who were causing the problem, that is, his valued colleagues, preferably in a way that allowed them to voice some frustration before ultimately sinking into the complete resignation that this situation demanded. Victor did so in a low monotone edged with irritation—as if he didn't entirely understand why he was being harassed with this morbid responsibility. Some faculty took the opportunity to protest the claims from the report that they found especially insulting, while others stared at the presentation dumbly, as if trying to deaden their senses until the meeting was over.

By the time Elena entered the room, Victor was already up to the slide marked "The Myth of Small Class Sizes?" She had had to park in the South Lot, all the way down by the tennis courts, which was nearly a thirty-minute walk away from the meeting, or about a twenty-six-minute sprint/trot for someone trying not to sweat too visibly through her clothes. When she finally arrived at the meeting, she immediately regretted giving advice to Francesca, the five-eighths in Portuguese, who was now sitting up front in Elena's normal spot. The rest of the front row was filled by the Spanish faculty, whose consistently high enrollments put them in permanent charge of the show. To the back left, the Germans had huddled into defensive formation—which likely meant that they had met informally beforehand to discuss their tactics for deflecting the consultants' report. German was the number two faction in Modern Languages, mainly because old bushy-browed Klaus had managed to secure two new tenure lines (one a joint appointment with English) during his time as Chair, back before the permanent renovations to the dormitories and campus center began, in that Golden Time when students came to college to explore new ideas and the State still considered investment in education central to its interests. Those two hires, Christian and Belinda, now remained as living testimony to this mythic time, as well as assurance of the German program's continuance into the foreseeable future. Carefully holding up her bag so as not to bump anyone's desk, Elena quietly slipped through the room tucked herself into the third row, making herself one vertex of a triangle with these two Germans. If she couldn't sit in the front row, she would at least cozy up to some tenured faculty in the hope of syphoning off some of their aura of permanence.

Victor next pulled up a slide labeled *Our Expenses Today*. "As you can see here, the consultants have separated all of the College's expenses into four categories: 'Attracting Students,' 'Building Community,' 'Preparing Students,' and 'Supplemental Costs.' I won't read the report verbatim, but essentially: 'Attracting Students' encompasses things like our new campus center and the recent expansion of our Admissions department, 'Building Community' includes alumni outreach efforts and expanding stadium seating, 'Preparing Students' covers the budgets for new lab equipment and raising the national prestige of our business and economics departments; lastly, 'Supplemental Costs' includes various things, ranging from water coolers (which we'll come back to) to—most notably—faculty compensation for Modern Languages. As you can see on the next slide,

Expenses at a Healthy University, they want the bar for 'Supplemental Costs' to drop as low as possible. So this will mean a number of things. Let's start by talking about how much water we're drinking…"

The water comment predictably started a heated argument, with some faculty members accusing others of taking more than their fair share, others rather dramatically drawing attention to this assault on their biological needs, a couple making more or less incoherent contributions (one of which bravely seemed to imply that proper hydration was really just a luxury problem for those who already had tenure), and the majority of the non-tenured faculty patiently waiting to see if the rest of the Chair's report would provide any hint of how to survive the coming cutbacks. It was during the water argument that Elena first noticed that Amrita wasn't in the room. Her absence wasn't unusual in itself, but it kinda highlighted the fact that she could have just given up the parking spot. (Also, Elena couldn't help mentally noting that despite retaining her coordinator position so far, Amrita evidently gave zero shits about the planning the future and cultivating the culture of the Department.) More surprisingly, Sandra—the five-eighths for French, —who took absolutely every opportunity to demonstrate how much she cared about planning the future and cultivating the culture of the Department—was also missing. Elena trusted Sandra even less than she trusted Amrita. Remember the French and Italian film series two years ago? Because Sandra made the screenings a required part of her class, they ended up showing only one Italian film, and it ended up being fucking *Cinema Paradiso* after Sandra vetoed Elena's "too violent" first suggestion and the College's copy of *The Bicycle Thief* suddenly went missing. Then, the Department decided to approve it as just a French film series for the next year, ostensibly to lighten Elena's workload—but who started the rumor that it needed lightening? Elena certainly hadn't been telling people that she needed less on her plate. There was something suspicious about Sandra, how positive and friendly she always was. Someone should just—

By the time Elena mentally rejoined the presentation, Victor had advanced to a slide titled *Anatomy of a Healthy College*. The chart representing a healthy college looked oddly like a squatting demon being showered with money. The legs were made up of "Tuition" and "Research Grants," which connected back to the main body through the "Office of Admissions" and "Faculty Research (STEM)." The body was made up of the students, who were represented graphically by small images of the campus center and the college mascot, Minerva the barn owl, dressed up in a football uniform with the helmet under one wing. The arms were labeled "Athletics" and "Student Employment," and they were reaching upwards to catch gold coins being dumped out from what looked to Elena like a chamber pot marked "Alumni." Of course, the misshapen head was made up of the President and other top administrators, but the box seemed to have been designed in a hurry, as its sides overshot the top and looked like little horns. Elena wanted to ask a question, or perhaps several question, about this slide, but before she could quite formulate one, Victor had already moved on to some bar graphs and pie charts showing the department budget. The sliver going to "Water" was specially highlighted on each of these graphs, and the room promptly erupted once more into a debate on water rationing.

The overall picture was stark. Water was just one of the things that the Department would have to cut back on. Photocopies, film screenings, invited lecturers... new hires... There was a wide range of regular Department expenses that would need to be cut drastically. For Elena, none of this was very surprising—there was always talk about new cuts in the Department. What she didn't know was whether this would affect their Italian offerings for next year. It really shouldn't: there was still student interest and, all things considered, rehiring Elena to teach two classes for another year wouldn't cost very much. But then again, neither did the water...

So after the meeting, Elena tried to catch Victor to ask whether he had finished updating the departmental schedule for next fall. Unfortunately for her, Victor seemed to have been endowed with a preternatural ability to sense an oncoming uncomfortable conversation and avoid its source. It seemed that every time Elena tried to approach Victor he had just started a conversation with someone else, and the moment she herself became momentarily distracted Victor managed to disappear from sight.

Giving up, Elena instead stopped by the department office to approve her time sheet for the latest pay period. While she was chatting with the department manager, Cristina, about how unfortunate it was that Sandra missed today's meeting, a student hesitantly approached the desk.

"Excuse me," he said a little nervously. (As much as Elena tried not to infantilize college students, she found it adorable that this kid found her and Cristina intimidating.) "Have either of you seen Professor Pandita?"

At these words, Elena felt a pang of jealousy. Amrita was evidently addressed by her students as "Professor Pandita," rather than "Ms. Pandita," or simply "Amrita." The only time Elena's students normally used a title for her was when they addressed her as "Hey Professor"...

"I'm sorry," Cristina told him. "Professor Pandita hasn't been to the office today.

CHAPTER FOUR

"You have to be cutthroat." This was a favorite phrase of Elena's adviser, Nieves, when lecturing graduate students about the job market. To a certain extent, the tone of this statement reflected its speaker's fondness for harsh rhetoric—after all, when giving students advice on revising their dissertations she often said with relish: "Don't hesitate to kill your babies." But Nieves also believe her unsentimental perspective on things was one of her main contributions to the department. On many occasions, she had criticized the senior faculty in French & Italian, who hypocritically (in her view) insisted on viewing graduate students as simply curious and talented young people who should make the most of this fortunate time when they could be paid to study.   They encouraged the students to pursue their interests for their own sake, regardless of how their decisions affected their future career success. But Nieves saw this perspective as irresponsible. These *adults* had chosen to go into academia to the exclusion of many other well-paying alternatives, and their purpose in doing so was surely to get a job—and not just any job, but the same position as a tenured Professor they had seen as undergraduates, with cozy offices, comfortable compensation, and a certain level of institutional respect. To get a job like this, it quite honestly didn't matter much how they felt about their studies, or whether there was another topic that would better "fulfill" their interests. It only mattered how well they could produce the kind of work hiring committees wanted to see. Sugarcoating any of this was dishonest and harmful. If the Department really respected their students and their aspirations, they would help them achieve what they actually wanted to achieve—and they couldn't do this by coddling them. The students needed to be uncompromising with themselves and those around them; otherwise, they didn't stand a chance.

Of course, Nieves's outspoken views on professionalization divided the

12

Department. Several students found it refreshing for a faculty member to speak so directly about a source of such great anxiety for them, and they especially appreciated the fact that Nieves gave them more practical career advice than any other faculty member. It was never a guarantee that her advice would ultimately work out—the job application process was essentially a black box that simply swallowed most inputs, while spitting a few back out onto tenure tracks—but she at least gave them *something* to try, at least *some* control over their futures. Other graduate students, however, were less enthusiastic about Nieves's advice. The least generous among them thought that she was sadistic, deliberately playing on grad students' fears for her own enjoyment. When pressed, however, most of the grad students would say that they didn't doubt Nieves's intentions, the real issue was that she wasn't sensitive to the ways in which the tone of her advice amplified the anxieties of her students, and the panic her words could produce was neither healthy nor productive.

Elena switched into the pro-Nieves camp after her first public presentation, at a small graduate conference hosted by her department in the spring of her first year. The discussant dealt with her paper in a few sentences: "As concerns Ms. Malatesta's paper, I don't really have much to say. I'm sure it's clear to everyone what she was trying to do. Perhaps she would be willing to tell us, however, why she thought it was worth doing. There's been so much interesting work on this subject written by," he listed three names known well to most of the faculty in the room, "as I'm sure Ms. Malatesta is aware. So I hope she can tell us why she decided not to engage with their work, and more generally, what she hoped all of us here could take away from her analysis." Ms. Malatesta was not aware of these scholars' work, nor did she understand why she needed to explain what they ought to take away if it was "clear to everyone what she was trying to do." She stumbled through a response and then sat for another thirty minutes as the other panelists answered questions, all the while hoping no one in the audience could see the rush of heat to her face.

While she was sitting there, patiently waiting to be allowed to leave the panel, she kept going over the details of her argument, trying to figure out where it went so drastically wrong. The discussant's comments clearly implied that her argument was basically accurate, but her work was somehow not *interesting* as scholarship. Of course, she had no absolutely idea what was lacking to make it interesting, especially since the topic had obviously interested her, and when she finally did read the relevant works by the scholars her discussant had recited, she still didn't understand what made their perspectives so much more *interesting* than hers. Nonetheless, she firmly resolved never to be in this situation again—either she would leave the academic community entirely or she would find a way to make her scholarship *interesting*. By the following fall, she had firmly decided on that latter course: she would learn how to do her academic work in such a way that it *had* to be taken seriously, and she would learn how to respond to criticism in a way that made the people who underestimated her feel humiliated. Naturally, this resolution led her to seek a closer relationship with Nieves, who formally accepted the role of Elena's dissertation adviser the following year.

With Nieves's guidance, Elena now jumped into the role of a Promising Young Scholar with total dedication. On any given day, there were few moments not devoted to work in one form or another. She even tried to read while cooking for a little while, but gave this up after the second time she burned herself making oatmeal. (Podcasts while cooking would work better when she learned about podcasts a couple years later.) Every trip out of the apartment was preceded by a short calculus based on the necessity of the trip and how far it would set back her work schedule. The only way she could convince herself to get more sleep at night was to remind herself that her brain worked less efficiently without rest. In terms of self-presentation, she worked on being firmer and more aggressive in the substance of her comments, while also training her tone of voice not to sound overly pushy or critical. She read everything she could find about how to dress as a young female academic and more generally how not to come across as a grad student.

As an adviser, Nieves was attentive, inspiring, and—exhausting. The great thing about working with her was that Nieves really invested time and energy in her graduate students, constantly encouraging them to step back and critically reexamine their projects from new points of view. She also seemed to know an incredibly intimidating amount about an exceedingly wide range of methodological and theoretical models. Every conversation with Nieves presented an opportunity not only to discuss one's work, but also to radically rethink one's entire approach to scholarship and, by extension, one's identity as a scholar. Elena found meetings with her simultaneously intimidating and exhilarating for this reason. In retrospect, it would have been difficult for her even to imagine her graduate life without these intensive interactions. At the same time, she couldn't help but notice her enthusiasm for Nieves's constant probing wane as she developed her dissertation, especially as she started to think about at timeline for finishing it. After a certain point she dreaded advisor-advisee meetings more than she looked forward to them.

The main reason was quite simply fatigue. At a certain level, Elena knew there was a lot of important scholarship out there she hadn't read, and she could acknowledge that there were more exciting and ambitious ways of conceptualizing her project. Still, at some point she had to focus on putting the ideas she already had to paper in a more or less coherent way, and she couldn't do this if she was always broadening the scope of her thinking.

Also, a very practical doubt had started creeping up on her: What if she couldn't physically keep up with the readings she felt she needed to do? There were just so many things already written, and more kept coming all the time… She tried to skim, but this felt somehow dishonest, and besides she was never entirely sure that she was focusing on the parts of the argument that Nieves wanted her to focus on. So she kept setting impossibly ambitious reading goals and then chastising herself for not meeting them. She was stuck in a vicious circle: the more reading she did, the more at sea she felt, but the more she was at sea, the worse was her desire to read. And this whole time, her dissertation wasn't getting written.

As she continued this cycle, the worst part was the awareness of the fact that she was struggling. At a certain level, she always wondered whether her difficulties weren't just a matter of assiduity and endurance—what if she actually wasn't intelligent enough to keep up with the demands of academia? Was the difference between her and Nieves, for instance, only a matter of hard work? Surely, there were people who had greater aptitude than others. So, what if the people who succeeded in academia were just naturally and essentially brilliant—and Elena wasn't? (Yes, she recognized the hypocrisy of believing this even though in every other case she dismissed arguments predicated on assuming some unchangeable "nature" or "essence," but this awareness made no difference.) She never expressed this doubt to others, but it was the motor for the spiral of insecurity and obsessive reading that characterized her graduate life. Of course, she had heard people describe the feelings she was going through as something called "impostor syndrome," but this didn't help. Who cared if other people felt this way—especially when those people kept being so damn smart and productive? The issue was that Elena kept falling short of her own expectations, and she *knew* those expectations couldn't be wholly arbitrary. Maybe everyone else irrationally feared finding out that they were, in fact, like Elena: Morlocks pretending to be… whatever the other group in *The Time Machine* were.

(Editor's note: At this point we are excising a lengthy digression from Elena's train of thought where she attempts to draw connections between her own life and the X-men "Mutant Massacre" story arc. Without judging the overall merits of this analogy, we find it unnecessary for understanding her state of mind during the events in question.)

Over the next couple days, Elena would have occasion to reflect on just how much she had lost control of her self-image during her time in grad school. For at least a large portion of this time, her primary goal in life was to become the person Nieves thought she should be on the basis of the aggregate expectations of hiring committees across the country. Actually, that wasn't quite it. If Elena were being honest with herself, it was an image based on her own anxieties about what these committees wanted, a dynamic aggregate of her own fears and inferences that evolved in response to Nieves's input. The result was a constantly mutating object of desire and panic—an impossible ideal that always looked just approachable enough for her to keep seeking it.

The only question she ever asked was: Would she ever make it? But maybe she should have been asking: How long until she snapped?

CHAPTER FIVE

After the meeting was over, Elena was pleasantly surprised to find the adjunct office empty. It was a smallish space, about the size of one-and-a-half regular faculty offices, with a desk along one wall and a round table in back. There were a few movie posters hung about the room. Two were Elena's—English-language posters for Dario Argento's *Bird with the Crystal Plumage* and Sergio Martino's *Torso*, both of which featured the heroine framed by a murder weapon held in the iconic black-gloved hand of a 1970s cinematic serial killer—and one was a Polish poster for Hitchcock's *Vertigo*, essentially a crazy-looking skull with a target on the forehead, which had been left behind by Raheem (a former adjunct in Spanish and fan of Polish poster design). At some point, Raheem had also made up an inspirational flyer consisting of the image from a Polish poster for *Rosemary's Baby*—a furry little hand holding onto its human mother—and the caption "Hang in there!" This flyer now hung across from the desk alongside a portrait of Marx, rumored to weep every May 1, and one of Foucault labeled "Knowledge is Underpaid."

Today Elena couldn't believe her luck. Usually the adjunct office was crowded in the afternoons, but she hadn't run into anyone there all week. And she could hardly believe that she had the room all to herself on a Wednesday of all days! For once, she didn't even worry about how much of the table her laptop took up or how long she monopolized the table space. She placed her little plastic container of quinoa, napkin, laptop, and cup of tea on the table and spread them out as much as possible. (Not wanting to overindulge, however, she saved the small bag of almonds she had brought for later in the afternoon.) She ate her quinoa at a leisurely pace while reading a quick article on the politics of retrospective canonization in the Italian film industry as exemplified by the legacy of exploitation legend Lucio Fulci without distraction.

After the annoying misfire with the meeting this morning, Elena was feeling fully recovered and even fairly productive. Maybe today wouldn't be a total disaster after all. In fact, she decided to check off a task that she had long been avoiding and make a quick (she hoped) trip down the hall to Derek's office. If she could pull this errand off, she could consider today fully redeemed.

Derek taught Spanish language and literature. As the Department's liaison to the Study Abroad Office, he also assisted in organizing the study abroad programs for the other languages. When he spoke with the language coordinators about study abroad, he liked to drop a few phrases in their languages of specialization to show off. He was working on Italian now and had hinted to Elena that he would like to have weekly Italian conversation sessions. Wanting to be a helpful colleague, but not wanting either to talk to Derek or to take on more unpaid labor, Elena had insisted that he borrow instead one of her favorite books, an old crime novel called *Il Coltello*, which had an abundance of simple conversational dialogue. Elena had wanted the book back for weeks already, since she needed to check a quote for an article that she was writing (that is, in the planning stages of writing; that is, mainly putting off writing) and this novel belonged to a category of forgotten mass-market fiction that no one had yet thought to digitize. Nonetheless, she was reluctant to ask for it, not so much out of an obliging nature as out of an aversion to going through the face-to-face conversation required to regain it.

Talking with Derek was always a complicated experience. He was a perfectly nice person, just… difficult. While Derek wasn't tenured, he had been at Bellwether a long time and had detailed opinions about everything that happened in the Department or the university as a whole. Sometimes this made him a useful source of information (as when one needed gossip about how departmental decisions were made), but at other times it was rather frustrating to talk to him, especially when he started talking about the students (whom, in Elena's opinion, he didn't understand much at all). Most of the time, his comments stayed within the bounds of courteous discourse, but there were certain moments, especially when he discussed female students and/or students of color, that made Elena uncomfortable. This year she had even taken to using the bathroom on the next floor down to avoid walking past Derek's office. But she had forty-five minutes to kill right now, and her body was fortified with quinoa. So it was time to give it a try.

Derek ushered her to an uncomfortably low chair, closing the door behind her. (He always kept the door closed when someone visited him, mainly because any given conversation was prone to devolve into gossip about students, and even Derek was conscientious enough to know students shouldn't hear this.) He was a big, bearded man, an athlete in a former life, who masked his constant complaining with colorful sweaters and a consistently cheerful tone of voice. His desk was cluttered with Bellwether memorabilia, including a mug with the school's ouroboros seal, a football pennant with the old school mascot, and a nearly life-sized stuffed barn owl in a varsity sweater. As she sat down, Elena could already sense she had made a mistake coming here. Although she could see her book tantalizingly hanging over the edge of the top shelf, she could also tell from his enthusiastic greeting that Derek would never give her an opening to mention it.

"You have perfect timing! I have a meeting with someone from International Horizons in an hour to talk about our study abroad programs. Have you heard of this company before? Apparently, they're new. You know, they might want to talk to you too—Rome is one of their locations, I believe. Anyway, we're trying to find a cheaper alternative to the Study in Berlin! program—it's really a shame, I like that program a lot, and the students who go on it really find it to be a tremendous experience, but there's just the whole money issue. So, we'll see what these people have to say. Anyway, why was I talking about this—oh yes, I was just explaining that I actually have some free time right now while I wait for this person. So, let's talk about whatever you came in for."

"Well, it's really just that—"

"Oh! You know what? I'm sorry, I didn't mean to interrupt you. I hope you don't mind—if you do mind just tell me—but I just remembered something. I think you'll appreciate this. This student—I suppose, we're not supposed to call them 'snowflakes,' are we? but I'm getting ahead of myself—well, this student in my Latin America class just emailed me about why he was absent today. And you know what? Well first, he asks me if we covered anything important today, which is, of course… Maybe he thinks that the whole world stops functioning when he isn't in the room—as if I'm just an automaton who droops sadly at the podium when he isn't there. Anyway, just guess his reason for missing my class? 'Was he sick?' Well, here's my response to that. Were you too sick this morning to send me an email before the class started? I guess consideration for others is a generational thing… Anyway, no, he wasn't sick. He was at a protest. He's part of some group protesting the Murray Otis lecture this Friday. Of course, you've heard about that whole—"

"Isn't he the one who advocates chemical cast—?"

"Otis advocates all sorts of things," Derek waved his hand dismissively. "And of course, everyone keeps exaggerating everything this man ever said. You know, when he said that thing about biological determinants, he *was* citing *actual* statistics. And that term everyone's upset about him using—it was just what people said back when his work originally came out. Anyway, this student wants to miss *my* class all because some student group he's in has declared an all-day protest."

"Is he in the Pride Alliance?"

"I don't know, maybe. It was one of those student groups that like to take controversial stands and get attention. I hate to say it, but I don't have a lot of sympathy for these oversensitive students who always want to protest when someone says something they don't like. Whatever happened to universities being havens of free speech? I just pray the administration doesn't do something stupid and cancel this Otis guy's talk. And I also hope that the students understand there will be consequences for missing class. Otherwise, everyone is going to start using the 'protest excuse' to get out of their requirements. Hell, I don't like most of the people who give political lectures here. Don't I wish it would get me out of class! In fact, I was just talking to Sandra this morning, and get this, one of her students tried to pull the same thing with her!"

"I'm sorry—Sandra was here this morning? I didn't see her at the faculty meeting."

"Well, I ran into her outside the library a little before the meeting started. She told me she was getting something from car—you know, she had to park all way down by the tennis courts—and I thought she was coming back for the meeting. But I guess something must have come up… Anyway, look at me boring you—what did you want to see me about? Or— you know what? Could we take a rain check? I'm due to meet with someone from International Horizons about their study abroad offerings in a bit—maybe I already mentioned that?—and I need to review some of our program numbers before they come. Anyway, thank you for stopping by. As always, it was great talking to you!"

Elena quietly fled.

CHAPTER SIX

"Welcome to Prosecco Professor. The Professor is now in the studio and ready to take your questions."

After finishing her meeting with Derek, Elena returned to her office to make the most of the remaining twenty-some odd minutes before her "special study," a one-on-one advanced Italian conversation class, began. This class was "special" in the sense that it didn't fit any of the existing course rubrics and so had to be registered as a half credit for the student and an "advisory responsibility" for the faculty member. ("Advisory responsibilities" were, incidentally, compensated at a *much* lower pay rate than classes.) Technically, as an adjunct faculty member, Elena was not supposed to conduct "special study" classes, but she had actually requested an exception in a written plea to the Dean since a student needed this course to complete the Italian major. The administration had generously granted the request, and as a result Elena was tacitly committed to offering at least two more semesters of "special study" after this one (if they kept her on for next year). After trying in vain to concentrate on some grading for Italian 202, she decided to spend the last twenty minutes before her student arrived listening to her latest obsession, the "Prosecco Professor" podcast.

For some time Elena had made a point of *not* listening to the Professor. After all, she was already living all of the academic frustrations people brought up on the podcast, and she already had a hard enough time preserving at least a tiny bit of free time uncontaminated by work. The last thing she wanted to do was to open up another breach for work to seep in. But Connie was an avid listener. And as with all things, once Connie was into it she constantly prodded Elena to give it a try. Last January she finally cracked and listened to the special episode "The Lecture in the Age of Mechanical Reproducibility," an interview with several successful lecturers about how they have come to re-envision their art in the age of MOOCs. Surprisingly, Elena really enjoyed this episode and quickly became addicted to the podcast as she listened to more. It actually felt affirming to have some of her anxieties about her job discussed in frank terms, and she really enjoyed Prosecco Prof's unflinching perspective on things. (She was a little like how Elena imagined Nieves would be if she had more of a sense of humor.) Over the next two moths she binged on the entire first two seasons.

A typical episode of Prosecco Professor was made up of two twenty-minute segments. Often, one or both of these would come from a set of recurring segments: "Adjunctin' Junction" covered issues specific to contingent faculty; "Don't Panic!" dished job market gossip sprinkled with tidbits of practical advice; "Psychopathology of Academic Life" dissected stories submitted (anonymously) by faculty about their everyday interactions with students, colleagues, and administrators; "Alt Ack" explored careers including publishing… There were also one-off segments like "Spectators of Marx," "New on the Anthroposcene," "Cybermen: The Gendered Rise of the Digital Humanities," "Homo Studens," and the wildly popular "Screw it, Today We're Just Going to Talk about Beyoncé."

In the latest podcast, the Professor was doing an extended version of one of her most popular segments, "Nightmares of Higher Ed," where she read true dream narratives anonymously submitted by faculty members on her website. For instance, one senior faculty member remembered receiving a Lifetime Teaching Award in a cavernous hall illuminated only by torchlight. As a berobed crowd looked on, eating cheese cubes and drinking wine, the dreamer ascended onto a pentagonal platform to come face-to-face with her recently deceased adviser, who held a glossy plaque and a giant cheque. It was only when she accidentally brushed the adviser's skeletal hand that the dreamer realized the whole ceremony was the culmination of an elaborate scheme to force her into retirement, and her severance package, as quantified on the comically large cheque, was considerably less generous than she had expected. A tenured professor from the Mid-Atlantic wrote in frequently about his recurring dreams of a zombie uprising on campus, which invariably ended with him cornered in his office, trying to defend himself with a desk lamp while regretting his vocal opposition to firearms for campus security. A professor of German in the Midwest dreamed she woke up as a male beetle and spent the whole night wondering how this turn of events would affect her teaching evaluations. Someone who probably taught Russian admitted that in the days before Commencement each year they would often have nightmares inspired by *Ivan the Terrible, Pt. 2: Eccentric Boogaloo*: they would find themselves lost in a crowd of black robes, so caught up in the pomp and circumstance of the affair that they didn't notice a deadly figure stalking them from the shadows. Perhaps the strangest dream on the podcast so far was one reported about a month ago: A member of a hiring committee had written in to say he dreamed one night that a supernatural creature with a circular head and deep black eyes had visited him to warn that one of the department's three finalists was a changeling determined to open a portal to Hell during their job talk, but the creature couldn't tell him which one. Quite a few listeners called in to say they dreamed of suddenly realizing in the middle of teaching a class that they knew absolutely nothing about the subject or had never seen these students before today.

Today's podcast reflected how drastically the content of these dreams had changed after the 2016 election. In one dream, a mathematics professor was grading tests and noticed that the top students in the class had uniformly written the single word "Trump" in response to every question. More disturbingly, "Trump" was marked as the correct answer to every question on the professor's own answer sheet. This led to panicked scene: The professor frantically worked through each problem from scratch, filling sheets and sheets of paper with equations, only to come up with "Trump" as the correct result every time. An administrator wrote that she had a recurring nightmare of calling the President in for a disciplinary hearing, only to have him insist that he couldn't have committed sexual harassment because he's "a great lover of women" with "tremendous ways of showing respect." Several faculty members wrote in independently to report nightmares that their student evaluations were now being conducted via Twitter. But the most frightening dreams were the ones in which the dreamer relived actual events from the weeks after the election: chants of "Build the Wall," White people proclaiming "this is our country now," one student gloating to another about imminent deportations, Nazi symbolism, threats of hangings, a line of White "counter-protestors" shouting slurs and threats at a gathering of mostly Black students and faculty… Prosecco Prof promised to return to the question of the post-Nov. 8 campus on a later podcast. For right now, she didn't think anyone had enough distance to analyze it properly. In the meantime, she wanted to remind everyone to take care of themselves and to check in with each other.

"Alright. That just about wraps things up for today. Before we go, let me read off the highest voted listener question for this week. Oh… this one's a little morbid. @WeepyWikiWatcher asks on Twitter: 'If contingent faculty were being killed at your university at the rate of one per day, how many days would it take for someone in your administration to notice?' You can submit your answers on our blog. You can also tweet them to hashtag ProseccoProblems—though you might want to go anonymous on this one. Prosecco Professor doesn't want to get any of you fired! Anyway, keep your head up, Weepy, and get off that wiki! That goes for the rest of you listeners as well.

"This is Prosecco Professor signing off 'til next week. As always, remember: you're smart, you're beautiful, you're definitely not an impostor."

CHAPTER SEVEN

Elena was still contemplating Prosecco Professor's question when she heard Sasha knocking on her office door. Sasha was the living embodiment of the Italian major—in the literal sense that she was the only one in the Department, and quite possibly the last of her kind at Bellwether, the way things were going. In an exceptional display of bad timing, Sasha had managed to register for the Italian major shortly after all publicity for this concentration was removed from the Department's website, but just before the newly approved reconfiguration of "lesser taught language" majors officially went into effect, and Elena had dutifully signed and submitted the paperwork to become her primary adviser mere days before finding out that her hours would be reduced the following year.

The existence of the Italian major was always a tricky subject for the Department, as it necessitated upper level courses, which could only be taught by faculty that the Department couldn't afford to hire. In years of fatter budgets and higher enrollments, it was sometimes possible to get approval for small upper level courses, thereby avoiding the dark magic of summoning "special study" courses. But even in better days they were sometimes compelled to strike such deals with the devil, and now the hiring for another part-time faculty member was out of the question, but they needed to do something about Sasha. So, with tacit agreement that the union would never find out, the Department allowed newly adjunctified Elena to teach an additional course this spring. To make matters worse, or at least more awkward for Elena, she practically had to beg the administration for this additional responsibility. She was the one who repeatedly went to the Chair and sent emails to the Dean in order to make sure that Sasha's registration as an Italian major—essentially, a clerical error in the Registrar's office—became a fully realizable plan of study.

The reason was simple. Elena absolutely *loved* Sasha. Sasha took Italian with Elena during her first semester at Bellwether, announcing on the first day of class that she wanted to learn the language because she liked Italian food and wanted to read *The Inferno*. Italian was Sasha's first foreign language, and she struggled a bit at first—Elena remembered that she appeared to be in a constant state of terror over class participation during her first two months in the class, and she nearly broke into tears after receiving her first exam back. But Sasha continued to work hard, pretty much commandeered Elena's office hours, and by the end of the semester became the top student in Elena's class. She was the first and only student to actually follow the ideal trajectory that Elena pitched every fall during course selection: Italian 101 in the freshman fall, 102 and Intro to Culture in the spring, a scholarship-funded summer class, 301 (now defunct) and another culture class in the fall, and most importantly, declaring a major (while completing 302) in the spring! More importantly, however, Sasha also proved to be the first only student to take an interest Elena's favorite movie subgenre, the stylized murder fests known collectively as *giallo*. Somehow during office hours one day Sasha let it slip that she loved American slasher movies, especially the meta ones that played around with genre conventions, and Elena immediately wrote down her online streaming password and the words "Soavi/*Stage Fright*" on a slip of paper. The registration form for their current special study said something about "learning journalistic Italian through readings and discussions concerning current events," but their sessions so far had covered *Short Night of the Glass Dolls, Don't Torture a Duckling,* and *Death Walks at Midnight* instead.

The subject of today's class was *Your Fear is a Crystal Blade Upon the Neck of an Autumn Doll*, an obscure psychological thriller from 1973. The opening scene juxtaposes shots of the heroine tossing and turning in bed with a gruesome murder on the Spanish Steps in Rome. After seeing a description of a very similar murder in the newspaper the following day, she becomes obsessed with the investigation, leading her to meet the film's main love interest, a reporter following the case. Several days later, she has a similarly vivid dream that ends up once again matching the details of a murder that had happened the very same night. She tells the reporter about her dreams, and he encourages her to see a psychiatrist, who then tells her that these violent nightmares are the result of repressed sexual urges that could be doing serious damage to her psyche. She has another similar dream, and this time one of her handkerchiefs is found at the scene. Only the reporter recognizes this article, and although he hides his discovery from the investigator, he begins to watch her actions closely, slowly forming the opinion that her "repressed sexual urges" may, in fact, be causing her to kill in an unconscious state. After another session, the psychiatrist insists on taking the heroine into his care, a suggestion vigorously supported by the reporter. Of course, it is soon revealed that these events were all part of an elaborate scheme by the psychiatrist to isolate our heroine, whom he plans to sacrifice to the god Mithras. The murder victims were all members who disobeyed the cult, and the psychiatrist had broken into the heroine's room at night to implant gruesome nightmares about the murders through hypnotic suggestion. The skimpily attired cult dresses the heroine in a loose-fitting robe and are preparing to sacrifice her when—

Sasha was running late for macroeconomics at this point in the movie. The library computer, which ran on an ancient OS, froze when she tried to fast forward. Since her special study was right after macro, she didn't find out whether the reporter swooped in at the last minute to save her or perhaps himself turned out to be a member of the Mithras cult. If Elena pressed her to talk about the ending, Sasha would imply that everyone died—that seemed to be the way most conspiracy plots worked out. But first she would try to avoid having to talk about the ending. Probably she could take up most of the class time asking questions about Mithras. (Elena always got exceedingly talkative when she didn't know something.) Otherwise, she could probably take up a good chunk of class time by making general comparisons to other films they had watched. If only she had made a list of vocab words to ask about…

Things were looking good when Sasha got to the adjunct office. Elena had her headphones out on the desk, which meant she was in a highly distractible mood. Sasha also noticed an empty bag of almonds on the desk, indicating Elena was also in good spirits. Sasha was able to burn up the first ten minutes of class with small talk, telling Elena about her new job as a campus guide and a couple facts about the guy the Humanities building was named after, who was apparently rumored to be a mystic and possible wife-murderer. (Or at least, so they would tell the prospective students; it was possible that they embellished to have something more interesting to talk about than his tenure as a dedicated administrator.) Unfortunately, that was the only interesting trivia Sasha could remember from her training, and so Elena soon started asking her about the film. Sasha asked to be excused for a minute, figuring she could look up a plot synopsis on the way to the bathroom.

The Modern Languages Department always felt a little empty in the late afternoon, but today was especially quiet. Sasha was startled to hear a loud crash coming from one of the offices followed by a strained groan. As much as she would have liked to leave the situation alone, Sasha thought it sounded like someone might be injured and realized that she was likely the only person within earshot. Listening at the door for a moment, she heard what sounded like labored breathing. Still hoping there would be a totally normal explanation, Sasha knocked on the door and asked if everything was alright. Immediately, someone called out: "Everything is fine. Thank you. Just rearranging my office."

Sasha didn't entirely believe this explanation, but she wasn't going to investigate further if the person in the office didn't want her to. On her way back to Elena's office, she noticed that the door was open and someone seemed to be dragging a large object out. Although he was bent over, Sasha could tell that the man was tall, and he had a shiny bald spot on the back of his head. She didn't get a very good look at the man or the object, however, as the moment he saw her, the man retreated back into the room and shut the door.

Now very curious, Sasha decided to check whose office it was. She was surprised to recognize the name: Derek Opfer. He had seemed perfectly friendly when she asked him some logistical questions about studying abroad in Rome next fall, so she wondered why he was acting so jumpy about running into someone while rearranging his furniture. She was also surprised by how tall he looked when he wasn't sitting at his desk. (Also, did he lose some hair since last year?) Anyway, it wasn't her concern. Right now, she needed to focus on thinking of something else to talk about for the rest of class, since the stupid internet didn't seem to know how the movie ended.

As it turned out, not knowing the ending wasn't an issue, since Sasha's interpretation of the movie quickly touched on a nerve for Elena. She was struck by the juxtaposition of women's bodies and the slaughtering of a bull when the movie depicted the rituals of the Mithras cult, and this scene epitomized for her a discomfort that she had felt with every giallo film they had watched so far. There just seemed to be something inherently exploitative about the genre. One could talk endlessly about the exceptional formal qualities (shot composition, scoring, etc.), and Sasha did really enjoy the visual aspects of these films, but there was nonetheless something very uncomfortable about the type of viewership they encouraged. It was as if the viewer was being asked to consume living human bodies with their eyes, and Sasha couldn't help suspecting that indulging in this type of consumption might have unconscious consequences in real life. She had an image in her mind about a giallo viewer who saw the people around him as fascinating objects, to be enjoyed and disposed of once they had served their function.

(Of course, Sasha didn't say all of this exactly. After all, she was a fairly advanced Italian student, but she didn't quite have a mastery of the abstract language needed for this critique. But she was thinking something more or less along these lines, and Elena could fill in the rest from past conversations about giallo.)

For Elena, this question of exploitation was always a difficult one to answer. There were aspects of the giallo genre that she found uncomfortable to watch—and there were certainly other movies out there that were much more gratuitous with female nudity and sexual violence than the ones they had watched. At the same time, however, she thought there was something valuable in it. She always found herself sympathizing with the victims in these movies, who lived in a grimy, exploitative world and often died for no better reason than a screenwriter's whim. They watched everyone else perish around them while holding onto the (usually vain) hope that they might prove to be something more than another mere victim: possibly a love interest, a hero, or even the killer…

(Of course, Elena didn't say all of this either. It would have been very strange to open up to her student about how much she sympathized with the supporting cast of a crime thriller. Instead, she told Sasha her ideas were interesting, embarrassed herself by asking some questions that were too advanced for a third-year student, and decided to have Sasha re-watch and discuss one of her favorite scenes for the remainder of the class.)

After Sasha left, Elena checked her phone for the first time since she had got to campus. There were two voicemails from Sandra in her inbox. In the first one, time-stamped about 11:27, Sandra wanted to let Elena know she was running a little late for the faculty meeting and asked if she could get Victor to wait a couple minutes before opening the meeting. The next voicemail came less than a minute later. This one started with muffled noises and a clattering sound, then more confused noises at a slight distance. Elena thought she heard a voice, possibly Sandra's, call out, but she couldn't quite be sure if it was a cry for help or just someone calling to someone else in the distance. The message continued for two minutes more, with only sparse sounds in the background: footsteps, perhaps, and someone saying indistinct words in a low voice. At the end, the footsteps approached the phone, and it went silent.

Elena assumed that the second call must have been an accident. Maybe Sandra inadvertently hit the call button while getting something from her car? It was a little odd that she had left the phone on for so long, but she could have dropped it without noticing. Of course, Elena still didn't know why Sandra hadn't made it to the faculty meeting, but there could have been a simple explanation for this as well. Some unexpected emergency must have come up while Sandra was heading to the car, and she must have accidentally called Elena while leaving campus.

It really wasn't that strange of a situation, but something about it still felt odd. Elena didn't have a concrete suspicion, but she nonetheless decided to stop by Derek's office, just in case he had stuck around after his meeting. He said he had talked to Sandra earlier. Maybe he could explain what was going on with her.

As she approached the office, Elena was surprised to see the door was open slightly. When Derek was in the office alone, he usually left the door wide open—all the better to ambush the unsuspecting colleague who was just trying to slip past to get to the bathroom. After a light knock, Elena eased the door open and was surprised by what she saw.

Derek's chair was knocked over and several things had been swept off his desk. A number of books had also fallen from the shelves behind the desk and now lay scattered on the floor. Also, for some reason, the room smelled strongly of cleaning fluid.

Out of curiosity, Elena knelt down to see if *Il Coltello* was among the books that had fallen on the floor. Instead, she found Derek's stuffed mascot owl—soaked with blood.

CHAPTER EIGHT

Elena was never entirely sure why she went to grad school in the first place. She was certain, however, that it had something to do with the feeling she got from sitting with three other students in an advanced seminar talking about Dante's *Inferno* at her undergraduate institution. A profession that valued such deep, thoughtful interpretation for its own sake seemed like an almost scandalous luxury (especially in comparison to her summers spent interning at various law firms). These experiences blended in her mind with a naive image of the Professor as the generic "smart person" in society: the kind of person who qualified as an expert witness, wrote books with puns in the titles, discussed their research on NPR, and made the cleverest of comic book villains. If the air of authority appealed to her, it wasn't *only* for her own sake. After all, she remembered all of the mentors that she had in her own life, how teachers like Marcello (who ran the *Inferno* seminar) had expanded her perspective and challenged her to think about language and culture in new ways. Although she superstitiously tried to avoid picturing her own future success, sometimes she would slip into fantasizing about sitting in her expansive office, flanked by bookshelves, across the desk from a bright student, who would never see the world in the same way after taking Elena's class. By a slow, steady process, the image of a Professor condensed in her mind, transforming from a vague prototype into a concrete picture of herself inhabiting this role—and although she understood very little of what this career actually entailed, she felt a strong desire to live up to this image.

Of course, she was also warned of the dangers inherent to this career before applying. After she had asked him for a recommendation, Marcello had sent her an email with the title "'Lasciate ogne speranza, voi ch'intrate,'" consisting of links to articles on the state of the higher ed job market. This was how Elena learned the terms "adjunct crisis," "contingent faculty," and "consumerification"—initially meaningless words that would slowly accrue ever more dire associations over the coming years, until any one of them was sufficient to conjure a familiar cloud of misery around her heart. Although these articles succeeded in convincing Elena that any reasonable person would see joining the academic workforce as at least a frivolous decision, or worse a willing endorsement of workforce exploitation, their work was undone when Elena followed up with Marcello in person and he uttered a fateful piece of advice: "You shouldn't enter academia unless you're sure that it's the *only* career for you." It would have been difficult for Elena to explain why the word "only" had such a great effect on her. Maybe she wanted to be the type of person who was *made* for a specific role in society. Or maybe she wanted to believe more generally in a society where people didn't merely have jobs, but had *callings* tailored to their individual potential. One way or another, Marcello's phrasing had kindled exactly the romanticized worldview he was trying to dispel. It also presaged a fateful change in Elena's relationship to that Professor image in the back of her mind: by imperceptible gradations her desire to become a respected scholar and holder of tenure transformed into a *need* to succeed in this career, an elevation of the tenured Professor to a universal standard of self-worth.

Once this thought pattern was established, it generated endless self-questioning and anxiety. If there were certain people out there who could *only* work in academia, a chosen group who were *meant* to be there based on something deep in their very being, then Elena needed to find some indication that she belonged to this group. Without being fully conscious it was happening, she started examining everything in her life to find these indications. Ultimately, this was why she panicked so much when she realized she couldn't force herself to read for eleven hours a day: it wasn't so much that she felt a need to read a certain number before she could write a strong dissertation, but at a certain level she thought of herculean feats of concentration as the kind of heroic labors a true academic should be able to perform. It wasn't enough to do a satisfactory job at a series of fairly challenging intellectual tasks. No, she needed to do something that was more than merely human, something that would show unequivocally that she belonged to the scholarly class. And she agonized over the fact that she evidently couldn't pull off such a feat.

Oddly enough, even as she constructed this mythology, even as she constantly judged herself a failure every time she fell short of the pristine image of a true Professor, Elena also constantly envied her friends outside academia for their wiser choice of career path. Because contradictions are generally helpless to block the progress of anxiety, she continued to harbor both beliefs, the cognitive dissonance only worsening over time. Maybe being one of those people who could *only* work in academia was really a curse. Maybe she should interpret her certainty that she was meant for an academic job as a sign that she couldn't succeed anywhere else. Maybe if she couldn't do this, there was nothing in the world at which she could really succeed. Her friends from college had other opportunities—they could actually help people as doctors or lawyers or high school teachers—but she could only study things no one cared about, and if she did really well she could publish some articles no one would read, in journals hardly anyone could afford, or maybe even a book that students could pass over when trying to find a critical overview of Argento for their term papers. The constant companion of her love for the academic profession was a loathing almost as intense. She felt the nagging doubt that even the job of Professor would be unfulfilling, perhaps even unethical—a form of social parasitism. But this feeling in no way diminished her desire to become one. Maybe in a paradoxical way it even helped to fuel it—the opposite intensities of love and hate played off each other stupidly and angrily to reinforce her devotion to this professional ideal.

Usually, Elena didn't think about all this. She just thought about academia in terms of the various tasks she had to perform in order to do her job well, and there were enough of these that she was always well supplied with distractions. But there were moments when the ugly mixture of desire and hatred at the center of her relationship to the profession became terribly clear. For some reason she always remembered a minuscule event from her first attempt at the job market: at a national conference in the fall, she had made a point of attending every panel involving faculty from the top school she had applied to. At a roundtable featuring a member of this school's hiring committee, she had asked an unnecessarily long and convoluted question that no one in the room seemed to understand, including the committee member, who stammered a confused response to a question much more insightful than the one Elena had attempted to formulate. It was essentially a nonevent, but she had nightmares about this poorly posed question for months after. Another time she broke into tears trying to decide whether going out with a friend to celebrate New Year's would be an act of career suicide (she had generals in two weeks!) or an affirmation of her autonomy as a human being. A large number of these ugly, revelatory moments would happen while on the phone with her mom, when in the middle of a long conversation Elena would start spiraling on the topic of academia—sometimes making an extraordinarily detailed case for the impossibility of landing an academic job, and at other times demonstrating that these jobs were easy to get and it was just Elena's own laziness/stupidity/etc. that was keeping her from succeeding. Sometimes she would just wake up in tears...

But the absolute worst demonstration of her emotional warping was when Connie had her job talk at Michigan. Elena was honest enough with herself to know that if her friend ever turned out to be more successful she would be ridiculously jealous, and so it was no surprise that Elena resented the fact that Connie had got a campus visit while she had never progressed beyond a first-round interview. What she didn't like to admit, however, was that she was actively rooting against her friend getting the job. Surely part of the reason was that Elena simply didn't want Connie to move. It was amazing luck (bolstered by local inter-institutional connections) that they had both managed to find part-time jobs in the vicinity of their graduate institution, and Elena would certainly be much lonelier if Connie moved away. But there was also a more disturbing reason that she couldn't keep completely hidden from herself. Elena was rooting against Connie partly because she didn't want her to be more successful. She didn't want her friend to ascend to the higher plane of the tenure track while she wallowed in a state of mere contingency.

If Elena's relationship to the profession as a whole was a big ugly mess of love and resentment, her feelings about her part-time position as coordinator and instructor were no better. She liked the teaching, for the most part, and genuinely felt honored to be the first guide many of her students had in closely encountering a foreign culture. But when she thought of the Professor, Elena invariably thought of a well-paid, respected, *tenured* member of an academic faculty. Although there were also more immediate concerns wrapped up in this issue having to do with salary, job security, and (especially) health benefits, Elena honestly cared more about the talismanic value of a professorship, its ability to confer a special status as an indispensable part of the Academy.

Of course, she knew that her current position could be a stepping-stone to reaching her goal. Yet, after two more years of failed applications, which really meant two more years of frantic revisions to her materials rewarded only by an oppressive silence from the schools that she had almost unconsciously started to imagine as her next home, followed by the reduction of her hours at Bellwether due to overall lack of student interest (though enrollments had gone up since her first year there!), it felt less and less likely that she was living the "stepping-stone" narrative. It was more likely that—

Incidentally, when she tried to talk to friends or family about how she saw her career prospects, they always tried to dissuade her from using words like "failure." Everyone who made it to this stage of their academic careers was immensely talented, they would say, and it was fairly arbitrary who would go on to a tenure-track position. But what else was she supposed to call it? For years of her life, nearly a third of her overall age, she had intensely desired something and made countless sacrifices to achieve it, she had endlessly visualized herself as inhabiting a certain role within the university, being a certain type of person, and now this was clearly not actually going to happen. She could shuttle around part-time jobs, finding other ways to supplement her income and support her teaching habit. Or she could start over in another career. (And it really was pretty much starting over—a PhD. in Italian literature didn't open doors in a lot of industries.) So, why the hell shouldn't she call it failure? Did using a different word make her feel less desperate? Was a positive outlook really going to fix the situation? Maybe there was a way to be more thoughtful or critical about all of it—she wished she were the kind of person who was always thoughtful and critical—but for now she was just going to wallow in the general shittiness of everything...

(This was actually part of the reason she adored Connie. Connie wasn't nice or positive about anything, or at least hardly anything. Some people didn't like that about her, but Elena thought it made life much more bearable.)

Once she noticed her thoughts had got to "general shittiness of everything," Elena would do the breathing exercises that the therapist had taught her during Grad Student Mindfulness Week. Maybe it didn't all have to be so dire. After all, she knew—or at least she thought she knew—that many young academic felt more or less the same way. She had encountered mini-confessions of "failure" on social media and at conference hotel bars that seemed to confirm others felt the way she did... But then again, these moments seemed to be drowned out by a constant parade of new publications, conferences organized, and inspirational teaching moments that her colleagues more frequently shared. She also noticed that many of the articles she found online about the emotional and psychological problems of academic culture included at least a veiled reference to how the author had succeeded despite these issues—as if sending the message that this article was written as a service to those without the grit to withstand this culture. She even had doubts about Connie's sincerity when she talked about her own frustrations with academia. Sure, Connie didn't mince words, but whatever she said still seemed suspect because Connie was just so much more successful than Elena (in the latter's judgment). She was smarter, wrote better, had made it further in the interview process—if Connie was also struggling, wasn't that only confirmation that Elena really couldn't make it?..

Another deep breath. Concentrate on the breath. Feel the sensations in your body, starting at the top of the head...

Of course, the problem with mindfulness was that Elena didn't like the way her present felt. When she focused on the here and now, she just felt vulnerable and alone.

CHAPTER NINE

The campus police station was a low, square building at the southwestern end of campus. Since it was in a part of campus less frequented by students, the grounds department had shoveled the snow into two jagged mounds, leaving only a narrow walkway between. As Elena walked between these mounds, she wondered if she should be heading to the campus police right now. On the one hand, her apprehensions about what may have happened to Derek were so vague that she wasn't even sure exactly what she should report—and she felt even less sure that there was something suspicious in Sandra's voicemail. On the other hand, if either of them really was lying injured somewhere, Elena wasn't entirely sure why it was appropriate to be contacting on-campus resources rather than, say, a hospital. Still, she thought stopping by campus police would at least make her feel better. Once she reported her concerns, they would become someone else's problem. Campus police could decide whether these were matters worth investigating, and Elena could go home with a clear conscience.

The sun was already setting behind the row of trees separating Bellwether from the interstate, and the dim streetlights were just starting to flicker on. Elena hated being on campus after dark. It felt lonely and more than a little unsafe, especially in the desolate areas around the police station or up by the South Lot. At least she could still hear students' voices near the athletic facilities in between. This din made her feel safer, for the moment at least. If she hurried into the building and made a quick report, she could probably make it back to her car before it was totally dark out.

Once inside the building, Elena was momentarily dumbfounded how to proceed. In front of her stood a large desk with a placard that read Campus Security and an empty rolling chair behind it. Otherwise, the room contained a rusty water fountain, some plastic chairs, a locked door leading to the area behind the desk, and an empty bulletin board. Off to the right was a dimly lit hallway. Since the chairs appeared to be arranged as a sort of waiting room, Elena sat on the edge of one for a few minutes, expecting someone to appear. When no one appeared, she tried calling out to the area behind the desk, to no avail. Next, she decided to walk down the dimly lit hallway, while noting to herself that this hallway felt much less secure than any part of the Campus Security office should. On the wall she noticed a number of old flyers featuring a cartoon barn owl's face and slogans like, "Be Wise to WHoo Your Friends Are" and "Have a Hoot but Remember to be safe." (Good owl puns were clearly in short supply.) There was also, oddly enough, an advertisement for the Murray Otis lecture on Friday, evidently titled "Preserving the American Nation." The flyer was professionally done, with a gavel in the foreground and, if you looked closely enough, some kind of fortified wall just visible in the background. There was a small picture of Otis in the corner of the flyer, and Elena decided that he looked like a shaved weasel but meaner. There was not much else to see in this hallway. All of the office doors were closed, and the hallway ended abruptly with a stack of chairs next to a lone desk under a barred window, through which Elena could see the sky was quickly darkening.

She decided it was time to get back to her car. And she was in such a hurry to leave that she didn't even look at the front desk on her way to the door, and so she was startled to hear someone call out to her.

Upon turning around, she saw that the desk clerk was a young, stooped-over man with a fixed scowl and prematurely patchy hair. By his demeanor, she inferred that he didn't have to deal with people very often and was perhaps annoyed that someone had come in during what he expected to be a quiet shift. Once he had ascertained that she was there to file a report, the man asked her to have a seat in one of the molded plastic chairs, as 'someone would be with her shortly.' As the minutes ticked by, she couldn't help but wonder why this young man didn't qualify as 'someone already with her now' and more generally where the hell the rest of the campus police were. Didn't they need to be here in case there was an emergency? Maybe she should have called the real police? But by the time they made it to campus she would never get home—and besides, it felt silly to call 911 over an open door and a small bloodstain. It would probably best just to go home and forget any of this happened… Elena was just gathering up her things to leave when a new face appeared behind the desk: a very rigid woman with short blond hair and rectangular glasses.

"Excuse me, Ms. Malatesta? I apologize for the wait. We have recently adopted a new protocol for filling out reports in order to optimize our response efficiency. Officer Daniels here"—the woman pointed to the stooped man—"has not yet undergone his mandatory retraining in our new procedures, which were recently suggested by the Moahil Loch firm to increase our efficiency. As such, he is not authorized to fill out a report. Could you please verify that we have your name spelled correctly? Thank you. Now what is your position at the College? Instructor of Italian? And is that full time? No, it's not an important question, but it's one we need to ask. Okay, and who is the person whom you claim was attacked? Two people? Is either a student? How about full-time faculty? Mhm. Do they happen to be union members? Well no, I suppose that's not knowledge you're required to have. I'm just following the report. We take every report very seriously. So let's see now. Do you suspect a student may have been the assailant? Mhm. In either case? Mhm. Were any students at the scene and somehow adversely affected by these incidents? Perhaps they saw violence or gore? Mhm. Just to be clear: were students involved in this incident in any capacity? Not to your knowledge... mhm. Okay, great. Now, what is your reason for believing that these two part-time—they *are* both part-time?—faculty members were assaulted? May I hear the message? Oh, that to me sounds like an accidental transmission, an inadvertent call, a—oh, what is that unfortunate name the kids uses—ah yes, a 'butt dial.' Officer Danube, whom you met, 'butt dialed' me just last week and it sounded almost exactly like that: some odd noises and incomprehensible talking. Isn't that right, Officer Dunbar? Hm... Where did he go now? Anyway, back to the matter at hand. How about Mr. Opfer? (How do you spell that?) Why do you believe he was assaulted? Well, a knocked over chair and a little disarray are hardly cause for concern - perhaps he was simply in a rush to leave. Did you bring this bloodied owl with you? No? Well, yes, of course, I suppose I understand why you were unsure whether to bring it, but this leaves us without much to go on. Of course, we will send someone over to Howlsley Hall right away to check for signs of an intruder. Just to be sure. Nonetheless, I would suggest that this may have been a misunderstanding. Perhaps Mr. Opfer simply had a bloody nose and was in desperate need to stop the bleeding. From what I understand, many academics are prone to bloody noses, that is, nosebleeds. It has something to do with the blood the gathers around the brain when it's being strained. You weren't aware of this? See! You learn something new every day. So yes, your report is filed. We are on the case. Now I suggest you go get some rest. Academics are also prone to anxiety, they say—Moahil Loch even covered that in their training seminar! Good folks, they really opened up our eyes to more efficient policing practices. It's a shame that Officer Downing, wherever he is, had to miss their presentation. A protected campus is a productive campus! as they say. You take care now. Would you like a mint?"

Declining the mint and deeply confused, Elena walked out into the cold night air. She knew she shouldn't have wasted her time with the campus police—though she still wasn't really sure whether she should have contacted the real police instead or ignored the whole thing. In any event, it was already completely dark out, and she suddenly felt very alone on the Bellwether campus.

The campus seemed to transform at night, suddenly becoming a less familiar, less welcoming place. Elena had only been on campus this late a couple times for film screenings, and she hated it. For some reason she always felt like the buildings had turned hostile, and after this meeting with the campus police she felt even more certain that she couldn't feel safe here.

It was roughly a twelve-minute walk past the now-silent athletic buildings to her car. She considered walking back to the center of campus and taking the better-lit path past the library and tennis courts to her car, but that would have easily added another twenty minutes to her walk, and she just wanted to get home. So she headed down the dimly lit pathway, where every other street lamp seemed to be burnt out and only the vaguest sounds of campus life drifted to her from the distance.

Sometimes when she walked around campus after dark, Elena thought she saw things move in the shadows or heard noises in the snow (the dark only caught her in the winter). It was creepy being on campus when there were no students around. Sometimes the light along the pathways felt like a spotlight, exposing one's location to whatever frightful beings inhabited the shadows. You never knew what exactly might be lurking just off the path, surveying the neatly manicured campus in search of easy prey.

For example, tonight Elena couldn't shake the feeling that someone was following her. As she walked past the athletic facilities, she thought she saw a figure emerge from the area behind the gym. She assured herself it was just a play of light, or maybe a student heading to dinner late after a workout, but then she kept thinking she heard something right behind her. It was a slight, indistinct sound. Maybe it could have been snow falling from a branch, or some other totally normal nighttime noise. But after a couple excruciating minutes she was convinced it wasn't just a normal noise: someone was following her.

She could see South Lot as a hazy patch of light up ahead in the distance. The snow cracked behind her and she broke out in a sprint toward the light. Now she could distinctly hear the sound of footsteps chasing after her. Not daring to look back, she reached into her bag to prepare her keys while sprinting toward the car. When she finally reached the parking lot, she made a delirious final push towards her car, which was one of the two remaining in the lot. She tried to open the lock with her remote, even though she knew the battery was dead, and almost cried when it didn't work. In her dreams, this was always the moment when she dropped her keys and froze with fear on the ground as her assailant loomed over her. But in real life her body worked exactly the way it was supposed to. She deftly fit the key in the lock, swung the door open, closed and locked it. As she turned the key in the ignition, she could hear someone beating on her window. She hit the gas, swung the steering wheel to turn the car around, and made way for the exit.

When she was turning, the car's headlights fixed for a second on the figure chasing her. During that second before she rushed out of the Bellwether parking lot, Elena could clearly see her pursuer.

It was a large figure wearing black from head to toe—black jeans, a leather jacket, and black gloves. But it was what she saw above this attire that frightened her most. Even though her headlights flashed across the figure's face only for that one second, Elena was absolutely sure of what she saw staring back at her: the giant head of a barn owl.

CHAPTER TEN

"Are you sure *you* haven't been murdering your colleagues?"

Elena often regretted going to Connie for advice. As much as she loved her friend's general negativity, probing intelligence, and dark sense of humor, these same qualities could be extraordinarily annoying, especially when Connie felt that Elena was demanding too much from her at the moment. And this happened a fair amount—Elena generally assumed that her friends would be in her corner no matter what happened, even when she was obviously in the wrong, and Connie had little patience for hearing out Elena's side of the story once she had determined her friend was, for lack of a more delicate phrase, being crazy. Once such a determination was made, Connie would refuse to engage with Elena on a serious level.

This must have been how Connie felt tonight when Elena showed up unannounced at her door with a disconnected story of sinister happenings on her campus. To be fair, Connie had immediately done everything a good friend would do: she had invited Elena in, heated up some frozen samosas for her, and listened to her crazed ranting for about an hour. But by the end of the hour Elena had the sense that Connie wasn't really taking her seriously, and now her friend was being a total jackass, trying to convince Elena that if something really had happened to her colleagues, then, based on everything she had described, Elena would be the main suspect.

"Maybe you have some kind of traumatic split personality thing," Connie said, dipping a samosa in tamarind sauce. "Like you hear a melody or see the light flash a certain way—oh! or maybe you had some childhood trauma involving snow—and now, whenever you see a lot of snow, you black out and start killing people."

Elena didn't respond.

"I don't mean to criticize!" Connie continued. "I've always thought you needed to let off a little more steam. If you were going to have a blackout massacre, you couldn't have picked better people to randomly kill than Derek and Sandra—especially Derek… Never met Amrita, though I'm sure you had your reasons for her too."

"Connie, I'm tired. Can you be serious for a minute?"

"Okay, I'm sorry." Connie paused for half a minute in what turned out to be mock contrition. "Let me ask you a serious question. When do you think the Modern Languages Department will start searching for Sandra's replacement? Would it be presumptuous for me to send my CV over tonight? Or do I need to wait for them to find a body?"

"Connie, this isn't funny!" Elena was angry with herself for laughing a little at this last question. She did have to admit that something about this whole thing that sounded hard to believe. It was even possible that Elena had confused some details or exaggerated the danger of what had happened today. But there was one part Elena definitely wanted her to understand: "Some crazy fucker was stalking me in the parking lot."

Connie didn't respond right away. When she did respond, she spoke slowly and deliberately, without a hint of derision in her voice.

"Um, so you say you were stalked by a crazy fucker in…an owl mask?" she asked. Elena nodded. "Okay listen, El. I'm not trying to make fun of you, but you realize that's crazy, right? No one dresses like that anywhere. There exist precisely zero situations in which a person thinks, 'Let me put on an owl mask to stalk someone.' And well… Didn't that exact thing happen in one of your stupid murder movies?"

"I thought you liked my murder movies…" Elena said, legitimately hurt.

"Do we really have to talk about this? I do like the Argento ones. They're like culture or whatever. But you gotta admit that most of what you watch is just blood and boobs—a killer who only stalks nude models because he's sexually repressed, a group of young female students who need to shower together to discuss the person stalking them… The whole genre is basically just a glossy PR campaign for male violence."

"Well, that's not exactly f—"

"But anyway, all of this is beside the point. Didn't the killer in one of those movies wear an owl mask?"

"Yes."

"Okay, this is the important question: Do you really think you're being stalked by a killer owl from your Italian murder porn?"

"Okay, it's not *just* murder porn. There's a whole—" Elena had to stop herself mid-sentence. She had caught herself reaching for her laptop in order to show Connie her detailed spreadsheet of *giallo* plots, which made clear, among other things, that the victims were models in only a few *giallo* movies. Much more importantly, she would argue—and Connie knew this well—that titillation was only incidental to the greatness of Italian genre films from the 1970s and 1980s, and—as she had written in length in her dissertation—the real point was not to revel in murder but to find perverse delight in the precariousness of one's own life. Indeed—Of course, Connie had already heard all of this, and there were certainly more pressing things to talk about at this moment.

"Yeah, I mean…Yes. One does have a killer with an owl mask," Elena conceded. At some level, she was happy that Connie remembered *Stage Fright*. It was one of Elena's favorites: a deranged actor escapes from an asylum to stalk the performers of a campy musical about a masked serial killer called the Night Owl. What was there not to love? Sure, the plot was a little rickety, but what's the point of having a well-established genre if you couldn't put some things on autopilot? And besides—Again, she needed to focus! "I think it's just a coincidence. This guy must have been wearing an owl mask for some other reason. I ran into him near the sports facilities— maybe he took the Minerva mascot mask from the equipment room."

"First, I can't believe your school's mascot is actually called Minerva." (Fair enough, Elena thought, that does sound a little made up.) "Putting that aside for the moment, you're telling me that someone dressed as Minerva to try to kill you—and his weird avian murder fetish just happened to make him look like the killer in a movie you've seen at least a dozen times." (Yes, that was what Elena was suggesting.) "Doesn't my split personality theory just sound simpler? You suffered some kind of psychotic break, murdered a few of your colleagues, and then made up this narrative of the killer Owl because it was easier to accept than the truth? I mean, it's either that or—and stick with me here—maybe none of this actually happened. You were tired and stressed, you were freaked out by a creepy voicemail and some weirdness in Derek's office, and you just imagined all this."

Demonstrably tossing her samosa on the plate, Elena stood up as if to leave. "I can't believe you're accusing me of making this up when I was just stalked in the campus lot."

"Okay, okay…listen, listen, listen. You know I care about you—and I'm sorry about the whole accusing-you-of-murder thing. But let's think about this. You came to me instead of the police. Do you know why? Because *you know* they would be at least a little skeptical that some weird bird man movie killer is out to get you. And because *I do* care about you, I'm not going to validate this delusion."

"You think I'm crazy."

"I think…you're overworked. Stressed. You spend close to twenty hours a week on translation and editing projects in addition to your course load, while also constantly worrying about your status at the college. You also have a bit of a morbid imagination and understandably got freaked walking alone to your car at night, especially way down in the South Lot. Remember when you thought Lamberto was trying to 'undermine' you for not citing his work enough in your generals essays? You were convinced he was meeting with the rest of the faculty behind closed doors to convince them to throw you out of the program. You even wrote an email to Nieves exposing the 'conspiracy' against you, before you - bizarrely - started 'confessing' that you were never good enough for the program and intended to quit anyway. El, if I you hadn't shown it to me, you might have actually sent it." Connie was staring at her intently. "I don't know what happened to you back there. But what you're telling me doesn't make sense, and I'm worried about you."

Elena tried to evade Connie's eyes. "I didn't hallucinate."

"Okay, well…Maybe you did see someone down by the parking lot. They really should have better lighting and more security down there—it's fucked up to make women faculty wander in the darkness like that. Maybe your imagination just filled in some details."

"What about the blood on the stuffed owl? That was real."

"Maybe campus security was right: a nosebleed. Or a paper cut. I don't know. But Derek's a big guy—it's hard for me to imagine that someone overpowered him in his office. Oh, and you didn't notice blood anywhere else. Wouldn't there be more blood if he'd been murdered?"

Elena had to admit that Connie's explanations sounded more plausible than her own version of events. Still, she didn't totally trust the fact that she was only imagining things, so she asked Connie whether she could spend the night. Most likely, no one had been stalking her on campus, but until she felt sure of that she didn't want to be alone in her apartment. After all, if they were somehow tied to the College, it wouldn't be all that hard for them to find out where she lived. Besides, she had everything she needed to do her lesson planning here, and Connie's couch was so very comfortable…

That night Elena dreamed that she was, in fact, the killer.

Even though she was committing the murders, she watched it all unfold without having the power to stop it. It was like watching a movie, or one's life flash before one's eyes.

Here was her car driving down from the seventh level parking garage. From the driver's seat she saw a woman with high heels walking slowly in front of her. It was and wasn't Amrita—she had exaggeratedly long legs and flowing auburn hair. Elena wanted to call out to this Amrita, to warn her of a suspicious figure stepping out from the shadows, but she couldn't utter a word. As Elena helplessly watched this figure walk toward her colleague, she saw her own hands grip the steering wheel until her knuckles blanched. With a feeling of relief, she saw that the figure was merely a diminutive school administrator rushing off to a meeting. Before she could exhale, however, Elena felt her car lurch forward. Time seemed to freeze, with Amrita trapped mid-turn against the backdrop of Elena's headlights, before the car left her crumpled body lying motionless in the pool of bright red blood.

Next she was driving down College Way to the South Lot. The rhythmic flashes of street lamps through her windshield placed her in a kind of trance. She felt as if she was soaring above the campus on broad feathered wings. She came to rest in a place that both was and wasn't the South Lot, but she didn't start immediately for the Department. Instead, she remained in the shadows by the tennis court fence. After a short wait, she saw Sandra appear from behind a mound of snow. Elena stepped toward Sandra, but her colleague didn't seem to recognize her—instead, she looked terrified and started backing away, only to take a somewhat theatrical dive right into the snow. Sandra didn't have time to stand up before Elena was already on top of her, plunging a knife into her chest. As she dispassionately watched her hand repeat this motion about half a dozen times, always in close succession with the shocked expression on Sandra's face, Elena couldn't help wonder whether she was stabbing her multiple times or just reliving the same fatal moment repeatedly. In any event, she was soon walking away from Sandra's discarded corpse, her blood drawing streaks in the snow.

Finally, Elena made her way to Derek's office. This time she understood what she was going there to do, although she didn't immediately understand why her right hand felt so heavy as she walked down the hall. There was something familiar about the weight, as if she had imagined this feeling before. It felt as if she was wearing a metal glove—yes, that was it, a clumsy iron glove with several raised points along the knuckles. Once she could visualize it, she knew exactly where it came from and what it was for. When she reached Derek's office, the door was cracked open, allowing her to see herself nodding along to his prattling from the absurdly low chair. The moment the other Elena left the office, the one with the iron glove marched up to Derek's desk and pressed the iron spikes into his wide-eyed face before he could say a word. She repeated this motion several times until his face seemed to disintegrate under her blows.

Once her business was finished, Elena washed off the blood, carefully stored the iron glove in the bottom drawer of the adjunct desk, and sat with a bag of cashews to await Sasha for their special study.

Part Two: Thursday

CHAPTER ELEVEN

For many, the genre of horror fiction carries an implicit promise of graphic violence. Although it is not strictly speaking a requirement of horror, which can subsist on suspense and slow-moving dread, many fans nonetheless count visceral shock as essential to the genre. One can see this impulse most clearly in fan discussions of horror films, which often praise movies for their kill counts and fault those that do not fulfill the promise of onscreen brutality. Many viewers even regard the ability to appreciate masterfully crafted gore as a sign of a distinguished palette. In this context, it's no wonder that some alarmist Christian groups have been known to allege that the mainstreaming of horror genres in the U.S. is part of a pagan conspiracy to indoctrinate youth in cynicism and disregard for human life. Even sympathetic observers usually must concede that horror succeeds by playing on our darkest passions and encouraging us to take pleasure in terrible acts—serving, at best, as a kind of release valve for pent-up tension, and at worst, as a morbid form of titillation.

As a genre fan, Elena harbored a deep hatred for such broad discussions of horror and its social value. She always thought that very idea of suggesting there was some kind of problem with enjoying horror emanated from a position of rank sanctimony. Yet she could never disregard this line of questioning entirely, if only because the "problem" of why we need horror came up so often when she discussed her research. While most of the films she wrote about were not exactly *horror* per se, the giallo genre has close evolutionary ties to gothic horror and relies on the many of the same sexual anxieties and gruesome set pieces as the American slasher. Indeed, horror fans in the U.S. often think of giallo as an artsier, slower moving predecessor of the slasher genre. So, even though Elena herself rarely ever questioned why these films were worthy of study, people would often ask her why she devoted so much time to a genre that was fundamentally exploitative, misogynistic, misanthropic, and generally incapable of promoting any positive social values.

When confronted with questions of this type, Elena would always have to suppress the first answer that came to mind. The very act of questioning the value of horror registered as an unwarranted form of aggression, a dismissive gesture intended to suggest that her area of research required additional justification to be taken seriously. She generally suspected a covert ad hominem criticism underlying such questions, as if she was really being asked, *What kind of person would waste her time on this kind of filmmaking?* Was it an implicit criticism of giallo as a vulgar genre, meant for commercial entertainment rather than serious art? Or maybe some form of ethical objection to the violence and/or sexual exploitation that defined this genre? Either way, Elena suspected a power play—the intimation that her research interests somehow lacked intrinsic interest in her interlocutor's eyes. Accordingly, she had to choke down a reflexively snarky response in kind, denigrating whatever her opponent, er, interlocutor, deemed a legitimate object of study. After all, this was precisely what was at stake: legitimacy. And to be legitimate, Elena needed a quick and clear way to articulate the value of what she studied.

But every explanation she could come up with felt like a massive distortion. The entire appeal of a good giallo, like that of horror more generally, lay in its rich and hideous ambiguity. Horror didn't belong to the order of ends and purposes, affirming morals or digestible meanings. It was a genre that invited the unformed, the uncertain, the unrealized, the unsafe. One that recognized that there were things that couldn't be put into words, feelings that couldn't be assimilated into a healthy, productive life, and fears that would never be overcome. All of this needed expression.

And Elena also thought it needed to be embraced. There was an enormous source of potential in the discomfort that characterized the horror genre, its propensity to unsettle, to disrupt the normal course of life. Any horrifying image or experience touched upon the unbearable, and therefore gave an impetus to change—not necessarily for the better—but in a fundamental way. Although Elena still didn't know how to theorize this feeling in a concise way that would satisfy her colleagues, she felt certain that there was much more potential in this discomfort than in any pleasure the genre afforded.

Sadly, even those who sought to rehabilitate horror too often fell, in her view, back on overly salutary explanations of its effects—maybe the experience of fear provides a kind of catharsis, a safe way to experience fears that would otherwise be paralyzing, or the genre should be honored for its capacity to perform a social critique by representing middle-class anxieties in exaggerated, demonic form. But the best movies invariably left the viewer feeling unsettled long after the credits rolled, and Elena adored giallo precisely because the depictions of social issues were always flattened to brutal oppositions and the explanations for the killer's motives were always completely ludicrous. They modeled a world that was defined by its poor functioning in the form of inept investigators, uncontrolled surveillance, sexually exploitative professional relationships, and arbitrary violence. In a world like this, there were no real heroes since the circumstances determining who would live or die were completely ridiculous. It was a world of pervasive contingency.

And here we come back to the response Elena was reluctant to share with Sasha during their special study. To a large extent, Elena was fascinated by giallo because she identified with the victims, specifically with their vulnerability at the face of stupid, brutal forces. If one didn't seem to have much power in the world, one might as well have a pretty face and a badass wardrobe. One's constant furtive glances might as well be beautifully shot. One's death might as well be framed dramatically by the camera. One's blood might as well come out in lush bursts, and it might as well define the color palette for the rest of the world…

Ultimately, the point of horror isn't to work through one's fears but to make them intelligible. At the end of the day, it's easier to live when one's fears are accompanied by vivid images than when they persist, legion, just beyond view.

All of this is simply to say Elena didn't feel *that* bad for dreaming about killing her colleagues. She felt awkward about it, sure, but she couldn't really control the associations her mind made when she went to sleep. In a way, she actually felt better after having such a vivid nightmare—at least, her fears had better definition now.

She also didn't believe that the dream gave any real support to Connie's joking suggestion that Elena may have been involved in their disappearances, though she did make it a point to get to campus early and check for an iron murder glove in the adjunct office. (There was none.) She also checked Derek's door, to find it closed and locked like normal. In fact, this morning felt like a completely normal day in the Department, a sleepy and grumpy respite before the onslaught of classes. Who knew? Maybe campus security really had come by and checked up on everything last night. Maybe she really was just overreacting, like Connie said. Maybe everything really was fine… Of course, it's always better to double check.

CHAPTER TWELVE

Sitting in her office, Elena thought again about the question asked at the end of Prosecco Professor's podcast. *If contingent faculty were being killed at your university at the rate of one per day, how many days would it take for someone in your administration to notice?* She still didn't know the answer, but she did know for certain *who* would first notice the disappearances and contact the police: the Department Manager.

Anyone who has spent some time hanging around academic departments can attest to the reverence generally accorded to this position. Perhaps the best way to convey the extraordinary abilities required of a successful Department Manager is simply to state that this individual is tasked with keeping a department running despite its being staffed primarily by academics. Even when no one else in the Department coordinates with each other, or even understands how to use an online calendar, the Department Manager gives the activities of the Department a semblance of being organized and under control. When something goes wrong with the course scheduling, the Department Manager knows which forms need to be sent to the Registrar's office and, just as importantly, *how* to fill them out. (In many cases, it will not be possible to follow the printed instructions literally, especially since the forms are not always updated to reflect new scheduling policies.) If *anything* needs to get done that involves other offices in the university, the Department Manager is the only person who knows which person to contact in each office—and in many cases the only one who knows what these offices do. In departments with rotating chairs, the Manager is also a kind living memory bank of departmental history, fostering a sense of continuity between regimes and providing a record of precedent to inform future decisions.

The all-seeing Manager of the Modern Languages Department was named Cristina Velaq. She shared a large office with a constantly rotating cast of student workers. This shared office abutted the office of the Department Chair. Although the Chair technically enjoyed a great amount authority over the Department, the position was not very popular among the senior faculty, and a new Chair was selected every year or two through a contest of guilt at a spring faculty meeting—which meant that Cristina the only consistent authority in the Department. Elena was always personally grateful to Cristina because there's no way she would have survived her first year without her constant support. As far as Elena was concerned, the bureaucracy of Bellwether was a mysterious, vaguely malevolent entity, which could only be appeased by the offering of strange parchments marked with various occult signs, and Cristina was a skilled practitioner of the dark arts who could teach her how to satisfy this frightful being. On a more personal level, she was grateful to Cristina for humanizing the Department through a steady regiment of gossip about the various faculty members. While she never said anything especially malicious, or anything at all when there were others in the office to overhear, when she was caught alone Cristina could dish with the best. In short, it was absolutely clear to Elena that if she wanted to figure out what was going on, Cristina would be the person to ask.

"Good morning, Cristina!" Elena cheerfully strolled into the office. She casually rapped her fingers on Cristina's desk, the way a hardworking instructor who didn't suspect anyone was abducting her coworkers might do. "That was a pretty impressive presentation yesterday. I noticed it even had Department budget numbers worked in—Did you finally teach Victor how to make graphs?"

"Oh, I don't think anyone could do that," Cristina chuckled. "No, I just finally taught him to tell me what charts he needed in advance. He actually sent me all the numbers Monday afternoon, so I had all of Tuesday to make the charts."

"That's a victory at least!" Elena smiled. Incidentally, she never really felt like she was making small talk correctly, but no one seemed to mind it as long as she kept smiling. Trying to sound as casual as possible, she said: "How about that student yesterday? Do you know if he ever managed to find Amrita?"

"Oh - that student! Yes, that was really shame. You know he was waiting outside Amrita's door for half an hour before he came over to the office." (Of course, Elena was there yesterday when the student came in and knew there was no way Cristina could have known how long he waited. But where was the harm in letting her embellish a little?) "I don't know if he ever found her. She didn't come in all afternoon."

"Didn't she have a class yesterday?"

"I hope not." Cristina grimaced and pulled up a schedule on her monitor. "Well, look at that. Let's hope either she went straight to the classroom or she at least told the students she was canceling. No one else came asking for her."

"Do you really think she might have missed her class?"

"Well…I don't know. Maybe I shouldn't be telling you this but there's been a problem across DHS." (The Division for the Humanities and Social Sciences.) "A lot of the part-time faculty just haven't been showing up this week. They haven't been canceling their classes either, and students have showed up in the department offices looking for them. One of the English instructors even forgot to administer the midterm for his class."

"Really? Why do you think this is happening?"

Cristina shrugged. "Maybe they haven't been getting their flu shots, I don't know."

Elena couldn't help suspecting that Cristina was keeping something from her, so she decided to press further. "Still…it's really not like Amrita to stand up a student. You know, I saw her yesterday morning. In the parking garage a little before the Department meeting. So she was definitely on campus."

For less than a second something unusual happened: surprise seemed to register on Cristina's face. Usually, she was quick to respond to anything someone said to her: Derek's tirades on oversensitive students, Francesca's continual odd non sequiturs, Christian's bizarrely long silences—none of it seemed to phase her. But now she paused deliberately, as if trying to decide what to say next. When she spoke her voice was firm: "No, you must have been mistaken about that." Then she added in a lower voice: "Listen to me. Don't mention this to anyone else. You didn't see her yesterday, and you haven't noticed anything unusual on campus." Cristina paused for a moment, trying to decide whether she should say more, and then leaned in very closely and added in a barely audible whisper: "This is very important: You are not safe on campus. If anyone tries to get you alone in a room, run."

Cristina stared at Elena for a moment with raised eyebrows and her head cocked slightly to the side, and then turned her attention to her monitor to indicate that the conversation was over. Elena tried a couple times to ask Cristina what she was talking about, but Cristina just laughed off her questions, telling Elena she had an overactive imagination.

Elena left the Modern Languages office in a daze. Normally, she would head straight to her office to prepare for class, but she didn't want to be cooped up right now and decided to take a walk around campus instead to clear her head. If there was any doubt before, Elena now felt certain that something was deeply wrong at Bellwether.

CHAPTER THIRTEEN

The second-year class on Thursday mornings was usually the most difficult for Elena. In general, morning classes tended to have a little lower energy toward the end of the week, and Thursdays added that extra bit of frustration over the fact that it wasn't quite the weekend. This second-year class was especially difficult because the group always had a weird dynamic; for some reason, the students were unusually reticent with each other, as if they suspected their classmates of trying to gather compromising information during class activities. Over the past year-and-a-half, Elena had tried every conceivable permutation of these students during pair activities, but she could never quite crack a way to make them more talkative. Of lesser pedagogical importance, but a much greater personal insecurity, was the fact that she could never seem to make this group laugh. She had gone through every type of joke in her repertoire—from cultural references to silly puns to casual absurdism to even resorting to slapstick—and nothing cracked a smile. It was as if they were impervious to having fun.

By this point, Elena had mostly decided not to worry about it. Despite being a bunch of grumpy, fun-hating stiffs, this class was actually doing a great job of learning Italian. Of course, there was some variation among members of the class, but their average test scores were consistently excellent. Even Teddy Soplica, who had seemed like a lost cause during his first year, had turned things around: he was suddenly coming to office hours and evidently studying like crazy. Based on all of her training in pedagogy, she could hardly fathom how they were learning without actually speaking in class, but somehow it seemed to be happening, so for the most part she guessed she was thrilled.

(As an aside, it is worth noting that Elena was never especially prone to mysticism, but in recent years she had become more and more resigned to the fact that her life was controlled by mysterious forces. Intellectually, she felt very certain of the fact that things happened due to empirical causes that could at least in principle be determined through close observation. But since her first year in graduate school, and especially during her two-and-a-half years teaching at Bellwether, she had increasingly relied on "well, I guess that happened," as an adequate explanation. Even after all those conversations with Nieves, Elena didn't feel like she had any real comprehension how certain hires came to be made. Despite her close observation of two different academic departments, she didn't really understand how most departmental decisions corresponded to their stated goals or comported with common sense. And despite taking multiple classes in pedagogy and closely watching her own students, she now felt *less* like she had any idea why some students learned better than others, compared to when she started teaching.)

Happily, today's class would be simple. It was all review for the midterm, and Elena had already made an interactive review game for the students over the weekend. All she needed to do was to plug her laptop into the overhead projector and…Shit! Where was her laptop? She always put it in her bag before leaving in the morning. Now she could visualize it sitting on the side table next to Connie's couch, where she had left it right before going to sleep. And then she had woken up telling herself not to forget anything in the apartment. She watched herself grab her wallet, phone, keys; she even remembered to grab the phone charger from the hard-to-see outlet under the chair. Next, she started placing books in her bag when Connie came out with fuzzy hair and puffy sweatpants, and Elena remembered feeling a moment of intense affection for her friend, who just looked so comfortable and huggable in this moment, before they immediately got into an argument over the best way to brew coffee in the morning. (Connie insisted on using one of those glass contraptions with overpriced filters while Elena stuck with a simple French press…) Of course, the funny thing about this argument was that Elena was in a hurry and didn't even want to wait for coffee; she needed to drive home to change and then get to campus early enough to talk to Cristina. Yet they had somehow just started fighting about brewing methods when Connie went to brew some for herself. But then they had argued for so long that the coffee was almost finished and Connie insisted that Elena take some in a travel mug, which she did—and oh shit, she had run out the door without getting her laptop.

The students were already filing into the room, so she decided to stall them with small talk about their classes so far this week. (Usually, she tried to ask some basic questions in Italian as a pedagogical tool, but today she just started in English, secretly hoping to start up a conversation that would bleed into class time.) A couple students confirmed that their instructors had canceled classes this week—or not really canceled them so much as not shown up. In general, the students were feeling burnt out and looking forward to spring break. The class was also not looking forward to the Murray Otis lecture, especially after it was publicized that his speech at Berkeley had plagiarized from the *Protocols of the Elders of Zion*.

While facilitating this conversation, Elena was discreetly accomplishing several tasks. First, she looked through her textbook and workbook for exercises they hadn't done yet, then she performed a quick search on the room computer for appropriate exercises in the companion website to a recently released second-year Italian textbook. About five minutes into the class session, she was ready to go. She was able to take up the next ten minutes of class time by opening the floor to students' questions on grammar for the midterm, then she assigned a short medley of exercises she had just found, and finally she had the students write a few sentences using a grammatical structure that had tripped them up on homework. It was basically a functioning class overall. And afterwards, one student, Teddy Soplica, even mentioned he would be coming to office hours today. (Elena had always, perhaps spuriously, associated office-hour attendance with students' overall satisfaction with the class.) First, he just had to stop by some other professor's office somewhere on campus to drop off some piece of writing—he was a bit of a chatterbox and described this part in unnecessary detail, though Elena didn't really pay attention.

Back in the adjunct office, Elena resumed her attempts to piece together what was going on. Last night Connie had almost convinced her that this whole thing was in her head, but her conversation with Cristina confirmed that *something* was up. But what could it be? What would anyone possibly want with part-time faculty at her institution? It did seem unlikely that someone was simply killing part-time faculty for sport. Not only did this seem like an odd group to target, but it also didn't help explain why Cristina told her not to tell anyone. Did Cristina's warning mean that the administration was somehow involved in all this? Or did Cristina warn her against talking simply because she didn't know who was involved? Maybe the campus police were also caught up in the cover-up, and that's why they didn't take her complaint seriously last night... The cover-up for what, though? She still didn't have any clear idea of what might be happening, only the sense that there were people who didn't want it to get out that something was happening, and until she knew who these people were, she had to be suspicious of anyone on campus.

Elena looked up to see a man standing in her doorway. He was tall, neatly dressed, and balding just a little bit. At first glance, there was nothing alarming about his appearance, except possibly the way he was standing. It almost looked like he was trying to block the doorway, which he could easily do with his thick frame. He held a black leather briefcase in one hand and was resting the other hand on the doorknob. His eyes seemed to look past her as he spoke.

"Excuse me," he said very politely. "May I have a moment of your time? My name is Ben Molche. I'm a representative of the International Horizons study abroad program. Maybe you heard we were on campus this week? Am I correct that you are the Italian instructor?"

"Yes. Elena Malatesta." Elena stood up but didn't approach him. There was something she didn't trust about this man. "It's nice to meet you."

"If you have just a couple minutes to spare, I would like to talk to you about our classes in Rome. I think you will be very impressed with our program there."

"I'm sorry. I don't have time to talk at the moment."

"It will really only take a couple minutes," he said, stepping further into the room. He smiled weakly, still looking past her. "Do you mind if I close the door for privacy?"

Even if Elena had not remembered Cristina's warning, the request would have struck her as odd. She managed to maintain a firm tone of voice: "I've just told you that I don't have time right now. Please leave."

"Look, I don't mean to alarm you," he said. Now he seemed to be mocking her, swaying the door side to side as he spoke. "I just want to talk about the study abroad opportunities we offer."

"Please go."

Wordlessly, he smiled—and shut the door.

"I have a student coming to office hours in a minute."

"This will only take a minute," the man said, opening a pocket in his briefcase. He started to remove what looked like a very ornate pen of some kind, when there was a sudden knock on the door.

"Yes, I'm here!" Elena called out. She pushed past the man to open the door for Teddy. "Please, Teddy, come right in. This gentleman was just leaving."

"Would there be a more convenient time for me to return?" "Ben" asked. "Perhaps I could wait in the hallway here until your meeting is finished?"

Elena explained to "Ben" that she regrettably wouldn't be free after this meeting or anytime later today. And once Teddy had asked all of his questions about the subjunctive, Elena made sure to walk out with her student, keeping in close proximity until she had made it down to the first floor of Howlsley, from which she would be surrounded by students all the way to her car. She still couldn't imagine what the conspiracy at Bellwether might be after, but now she had no doubt that "Ben" was somehow involved.

CHAPTER FOURTEEN

Elena texted Connie from the car to let her know they were getting lunch. If there really was some kind of a conspiracy to make part-time faculty disappear in DHS, she would need someone to help her figure out how to survive it. And if there *wasn't* a conspiracy, she needed someone rational and brutally honest to talk her down. She was sure that Connie could meet at least this last requirement.

So she sped over to Wanesdale College. Half the visitors' lot was covered in heaps of snow, leaving no open spaces. Cursing her timing, Elena wedged her Civic in an indentation in one of the snow heaps, judging it to be unlikely that they would bother to dig out room for a tow truck. (She might as well risk a ticket.) As it was still thirty minutes before Connie would be finished teaching, Elena hurried over to wait outside her classroom.

Due to unusually high enrollments, Second-Semester French had been moved this semester to a small lecture hall in the Life Sciences building. This was a beautifully designed facility with an attractive reading library illuminated by skylights, lecture halls outfitted with all the best multimedia equipment from five years ago, and an alluring entryway specially designed to look like some kind of space age mollusk.

While she waited for Connie, Elena pulled out her phone to research information about International Horizons. The initial results confirmed her suspicions: the organization appeared to have no official website, nor could she find any discussion of them online. As she was still searching her phone, Elena saw out of the corner of her eye a slender woman with blond hair emerging from beneath the mollusk. Although there was something unfamiliar about they way she was carrying herself, Elena immediate recognized the woman's rectangular green glasses, visible overbite, and tailored gray blazer. "Sandra!" she called out, "Hey, Sandra!" But the woman continued walking as if she didn't hear. Wherever she was going, this woman seemed to be in a hurry to get there. Elena thought about running after her, but before she had a chance Connie had already walked out besides her. "Um, sure. Let's get lunch," Connie said, without slowing down or even turning her head in Elena's direction.

As usual when Elena visited Wanesdale, they went to the lower level of Clements, where there was an affordable cafeteria for faculty members. As usual, Elena made a small plate of beet salad and tabbouleh from the salad bar, while Connie piled every kind of meat she could find into a delicious pyramid. By the time they had paid and sat down, Elena was bursting to recount all of the strange events that had happened.

"I was right. There's something weird happening at Bellwether. I don't know what it is exactly, but there's suddenly faculty missing from all of the humanities departments."

"Missing? What do you mean?"

"Gone. They've disappeared over the last few days."

"Elena," Connie looked very serious. "This is very important. Pay attention."

Elena looked back at her wide eyes, half expecting Connie to give her a hint the way Cristina had. Maybe Elena was the only person left who wasn't somehow involved in what was going on?

"Are you listening?" Connie searched for Elena's eyes. "How much did you sleep last night? Have you eaten anything since you left my place?"

Suddenly realizing that Connie didn't have any idea what was going on, Elena was desperate to convey to her that she might be in danger. "This is serious. Some weirdo came by my office today, claiming to represent the International Horizons study abroad program. But I checked on my phone on the way over here: There's no program with that name. And Cristina, our department manager, had warned me earlier in the day that someone would try to get me alone in a room. Thank God Teddy—"

"Okay, slow down," Connie said, poking her pile of meat with her fork. "I'm having trouble following you."

"Look. This weird guy came to my office, tried to get me to sit alone with him. He said he was from something called International Horizons. Like it was some kind of study abroad program. But there's no record of them anywhere on the internet. And—"

Connie noticed that Elena was looking past her. She followed her friend's gaze to see a pretty young Indian woman with a stud in her nose and red highlights in her hair eating Greek yogurt a few tables down. "Hang on one second," Elena said, getting up from her chair. "I'll be right back."

Connie watched Elena walk over to the woman and apprehensively address her. After a brief exchange of confused stares, the two seemed to get into some kind of argument, and Connie went over to see what was going on. The woman with the highlights was gathering up her yogurt and calculus textbook, while Elena shouted something like, "Come on, Amrita. I know it's you!" to which the woman shouted, "My name isn't Amrita! It's Heather. Please, can you just leave me alone?" Elena gave a mostly incoherent response that ended in a reassertion of the claim that the woman's name was Amrita. The woman was clearly becoming very distressed and continued to insist on being Heather. At this point, Connie had made it over to the table and was apologizing profusely for her friend, explaining that Elena isn't usually...like this, and that he had been an unusually stressful day. Heather gathered up her things and hurried away.

Back at the table, Connie and Elena sat in silence for a few minutes. Connie couldn't think of a good way to bring up how insane that entire exchange looked. She had never actually met Amrita herself, but she was willing to take this woman's word that she didn't know Elena. So why was Elena so certain that she recognized her? Also... Should she bring up with Elena that it was at least a little awkward that she had conflated a total stranger with her Indian coworker? This Amrita was likely the only Indian person Elena knew—after all, the vast majority of her friends in grad school had been White, and she didn't really seem to have any new ones now. So there was at least a whiff of racism in this whole encounter... But then again, maybe she could give Elena a pass on this one? After all, whatever was going on with her was starting to look increasingly like an Oliver Sacks-type cognitive disorder, so maybe she should just be happy that Elena didn't mistake the woman for an article of clothing... Once Elena had recovered from whatever this was, Connie could talk to her about expanding her friend group further, but for right now she needed to focus on getting her off the conspiracy theories.

On her end, Elena couldn't think of a non-crazy-sounding way to explain her conviction that this *was* Amrita. The hair, the voice, the broadly curving eyebrows, the downturned nose: it was definitely her. Of course, Elena couldn't explain how Amrita had kept it a secret that she apparently also taught calculus at Wanesdale—nor did she have any idea why she had lied for years about being lactose intolerant—but it had to be somehow connected to the disappearances, the Owl Man, the bloody stuffed animal, the false study abroad marketer, and Sandra also appearing at Wanesdale. Could it have something to do with that consulting firm at Bellwether? According to Victor's presentation, they had talked about more effectively relocated intellectual resources—what if that meant some kind of aggressive retraining program, transferring faculty members from less in-demand positions to others? Maybe Amrita was trying to keep her second job at Wanesdale a secret from everyone at Bellwether for some reason? Or maybe it was something else... She just knew that something was going on, and if she was going to figure it out, someone *had* to believe her.

"Look, Connie, I know this all sounds crazy—"

"What was the name of the study abroad program?" Connie asked softly. "The man who came to your office, what program did he represent?"

"International Horizons."

Connie slowly reached into her bag and pulled out a brochure with the company name International Horizons written in big letters. "They were handing these out here yesterday," she said, placing the brochure on the table.

Elena looked through it. Sure enough, it looked like a real study abroad brochure: there were pictures of students posing by the Eiffel Tower and that little pyramid thing outside the Louvre; there were bullet point lists of program offerings and pricing; and there were a handful of vaguely inspirational slogans about cultural interchange and self-discovery.

"The representative said that they were a relatively new company and trying to make their name more widely known. Apparently, their website has been down for almost a month now, and they're worried that they won't get enough students." Elena still appeared to be skeptical. "According to the address on this brochure, their main office is just up Prospect, in Hatchers Hole. They must have sent reps to all the institutions nearby." Elena still wasn't saying anything, and Connie started to sound frustrated. "Look, it's just a new company trying to do some outreach. There's no big conspiracy here."

Elena was admittedly thrown by the brochure. It did look like International Horizons was a real company, and that guy who came by her office may have worked for them. But there was still something creepy about the way he was acting. "Look, Connie, you have to believe me about this. They took Derek last night. They came for me today." Her last card: "I need you on my side right now."

"El, you sound fucking crazy right now." Connie took a breath, hoping to sound less angry. "You need to let this go. There isn't anything sinister going on. You just… need to get some rest."

Elena didn't respond. She wanted to say something along the lines of, 'I don't care what seems plausible right now. I just need you to believe me. I know it isn't fair to you, but a line has been drawn in the world, and I need you not to think, but to declare yourself on my side.' But she couldn't quite form these words right now. Connie's utter disbelief gnawed at her confidence, and it was difficult to come up with an explanation for the brochure, if International Horizons didn't exist. At this point, Elena wasn't sure which she feared more—the actual existence of some strange conspiracy at her work or the realization that she managed to invent this whole thing.

CHAPTER FIFTEEN

There were some days when Elena didn't want to teach her classes. Truth be told, there were a lot of days like that, though she didn't like to admit it.

Elena had spent years listening to friends and colleagues rave about their students. One of the grad students in her cohort even claimed that he didn't like calling teaching his "job," as he was grateful to have such a wondrous opportunity to speak with intelligent, fascinating young minds, and the fact that he could receive pay for this activity was merely a miraculous coincidence. Another student would often loudly question how she would get through the week without the "high" of teaching. (After Elena's first semester at Bellwether, she couldn't help but wonder if this hopeful young teacher realized it was possible to overdose.) Very often, when Elena went by the graduate lounge during the late morning, she would overhear one of the TAs for French or Italian talking about what amazing progress their students were making or recounting some clever and/or complicated activity they had used in class…And all this was great, of course. Elena was happy that students were doing well and everyone seemed to love teaching. But she did not love constantly hearing about how well everyone was doing. Teaching was definitely a job to her—one she liked, sure, one she even loved most of the time, but not something that could in any way be confused with recreation. It was difficult, it was exhausting, it was annoying. And as much as she loved her students, they could be annoying too. She wished that she could ride some natural "high" of enthusiasm over all the difficulties—indeed, she felt guilty that she didn't feel this way—but this wave of uncut motivational pleasure never came.

If truth be told, Elena was an introvert. She knew from experience that she could teach an awesome, inspiring class under the right conditions, but most days it took some serious effort to get herself into the classroom at all. Sometimes, she even felt a nearly paralyzing sense of intimidation at the very prospect of standing before college students in a position of authority.

How could she ever live up to the legacy of her own teachers, people like Marcello, who had inspired her to a more intense intellectual life than she ever imagined before coming to college?.. As strange as it may sound, sometimes after long breaks from the classroom Elena experienced the petrifying fear that she may have completely forgotten to teach. Toward the end of a summer vacation dedicated primarily to research, she usually felt at a loss to remember how exactly she ever went about preparing for classes... And of course, there were also the frozen, congested mornings in December, when sick and exhausted from many long weeks of teaching, she would struggle to get out of bed for the last few classes in the semester...

In short, teaching was something Elena often needed to force herself to do, and there were many occasions when she just didn't feel up to facing the expectant stare of her students. So she had made a simple, ironclad rule for herself: Any day she could physically make it to campus, she would teach her classes. This rule may have occasionally undermined Student Health's efforts to contain the flu, but it succeeded in fully eradicating the question, "Do I have to teach today?" from her mind.

This is why Elena now returned to campus to teach her first-year Italian class, even though all evidence seemed to suggest that she had just suffered a nervous breakdown. If she were still convinced that there was someone stalking her, she *most likely* would have canceled this class. But she felt humiliated after her conversation with Connie and was starting to believe that this whole thing might have been in her head. Maybe she had overreacted to a couple slightly odd events yesterday and then started imagining things. To be completely honest, she knew that Connie was right about her reasoning under stress—sometimes, during especially rough weeks at work her thought patterns had become questionable to say the least. Whenever she had the impression that things weren't going her way, her thinking could quickly become petty, myopic, suspicious, and frankly embarrassing. It was entirely plausible that she was just being paranoid about this whole thing. So if she canceled class today, it would be her fault for not taking better care of herself, and in her mind this meant that she wasn't tough enough to be a good teacher. So the only answer was to overcome these vague fears and suspicions and to teach an amazing language class.

The first-year class today was even smaller than usual. When Elena asked about the missing students, one of those present suggested that several of them might be involved in the anti-Otis protests taking place on campus. There was some kind of "town hall" event, organized by anti-Otis protestors, happening on one of the quads today. The student protestors were taking questions from their peers about their stance while also providing a forum for those who felt marginalized by Otis's speech to voice their concerns. Although Elena found it hard to imagine the crazily young students in her introductory class engaged in any political action (again, the struggle not to infantilize!), she was impressed with their dedication and excited at the outburst of student activism at Bellwether, which had always struck her as a depressingly unengaged campus. (On a pedagogical note, she was also relieved to see that the missing students were all among those with the best attendance records, meaning it would be easy to catch them up on today's material.) In fact, Elena decided to stop by the event when her class was over to see this student activism in action—and maybe to clear her head a little bit by getting her mind off International Horizons.

The town hall was being held outside the Charles Duane Botkin dormitory on the east side of campus. When Elena arrived, the crowd was already thinning out, and the remnants of the event were fairly depressing. The weather had warmed up enough today that the remaining students were standing in a field of mud left by the melted snow. There were evidently no other faculty at the event; the only other non-student Elena noticed was the campus security officer with bad posture she had met yesterday, who seemed to be looking for someone in the crowd. Elena caught a brief exchange between two student speakers on the limits of free speech, but at this point they sounded like they were rehashing arguments they had already made many times. There were still some students who cheered when their side made a strong point, but the audience got smaller by the minute and the remaining crowd looked more and more restless. Soon enough, the organizers thanked everyone and started packing up their signs to leave.

While watching the crowd dissipate, Elena recognized several of her students. "Luciano" and "Massimo" (Luke and Maxwell) from her first-year class were both helping to clean up. Sasha was standing by the dorm entrance and talking to one of the organizers. In the exiting crowd, Elena noticed one of her former film students, Solange, walking away in a dining hall cap.

Although she was disappointed to miss whatever debate the students had set up, Elena was glad to have this reminder that her students lived full lives outside their academic work. It was so easy to reduce their whole being to the small slice that she saw in the classroom, but here they were spontaneously engaging in public debate to shape the culture of their campus. Of course, it was a little sad that this debate had to be about a pompous weasel person like Otis, whose views were roughly as defensible as a troll drunkenly writing online comments to a music video. But it was exciting to see her students finally engaged with an issue, and certainly giving the topic more discussion than whoever invited this clown to speak...

Elena was so caught up in romanticizing the simple fact that her students cared about things that she had already walked to her car before remembering that she needed to get the second-year textbook from her office.

The Department office was near the elevator, in the direction opposite the adjunct office. When Elena stepped out onto the third floor, the study abroad recruiter from earlier today was standing just outside this office. Apologizing profusely for his rudeness earlier, he explained that he was only being so insistent because he had promised Derek that he would speak with Elena during the short window of time when he would be on campus and he was afraid of missing his opportunity. Thankfully, his appointments for this afternoon had been postponed and he had time to talk now, if Elena could spare a few minutes.

By this point, Elena was mostly convinced that her earlier fears about International Horizons were somewhat overblown. After speaking with Connie and spending a fairly normal afternoon on her own campus, she felt more or less ready to admit that she must have been imagining things earlier. So, employing the fake smile that always served her so well for small talk, Elena apologized for her curtness earlier and agreed to meet with him right away. He would just have to wait one minute, as she could hear that Cristina was trying to get her attention. Elena suggested that—what was his name again?—oh yes, Ben; once again, it's very nice to meet you!—Ben should wait for her down by her office. Oh, he would prefer to wait right here? Of course, that was fine; she would be right back.

"Elena!" Cristina called out from the Department office. "Come here for a minute. You never signed your timesheet for this week. Here, let me get it for you." This was strange because Elena was sure she had signed her timesheet yesterday. It was also odd that Cristina offered to grab the timesheet since the mailboxes were right by the office entrance, and stranger still that Elena was certain the timesheet Cristina grabbed wasn't from her own mailbox but from the one next to it. Yet there was something about Cristina's demeanor that told her not to correct the mistake. After loudly thanking Cristina for remembering, she noticed that a post-it affixed to the paper. If she'd had time to think about it, she would have been surprised at her own presence of mind in this moment. After quickly reading the note, she deftly removed it while signing her name to the incorrect timesheet and tucked it into Cristina's hand while returning her pen. Cristina thanked her and made a loud comment about the unusually warm weather, as Elena walked back out of the office to meet Ben with an even bigger smile.

Cristina's note to her had contained just a single word:
"RUN"

CHAPTER SIXTEEN

Adrenaline always helped Elena survive academic conferences. She felt awkward in most social interactions, and it only made things worse to think that her small talk with colleagues might affect her eventual success or failure in an academic career. In fact, she may have never gone to grad school if she had realized that social interactions would make up such a large part of an academic career. Of course, she knew that there would be teaching and advising, but she was also excited for those parts of the job, and she hoped that her enthusiasm for these tasks would help her through the awkwardness. But it turned out that these tasks were only the tip of the iceberg. Every conference or workshop carried a whole array of potentially important social interactions (or micro-opportunities for self-presentation as Nieves called them) that needed to be handled carefully in order to cultivate beneficial relationships. (Although she had never gone through one, Elena couldn't help thinking about the social marathon known as the campus visit with absolute terror.) It was the fear itself that helped her get through. When she entered the conference lobby, she would get a burst of adrenaline that carried her through the receiving line of semi-acquaintances.

Now she needed the adrenaline to get her out of the building. Elena thought that while she was in the office she had seen Ben remove something from his bag. She wasn't entirely sure, but she thought it might be the same fancy, pen-like implement from before. Maybe a syringe? Whatever it was, it had allowed him to subdue Derek earlier, and she was much smaller than Derek. He positioned himself between her and the elevator as they walked past in the direction of her office. Elena wasn't sure that she could outrun him to the stairwell down the hall, or that there would be anyone still around on that side of the building. In order to buy time, she did what she had learned to do to survive difficult situations: she made small talk.

"Again, I'm sorry about before. How long have you been working at International Horizons?"

"This is just my second year. We're a fairly new company."

"And your main office is local?"—"Yes. Right up Prospect Pike."—"Oh, that's a nice area.—I'm sorry. Just give me one moment to find my keys.—You must like it up there?"—"Yeah, it's nice."—"Now, where did I put…" In the corner of her eye, Elena could see the Department's student worker, Alicia, making her way toward the elevator from the office. This seemed like an opportunity to try a different strategy. "You know what?" she said. "I would love to talk over coffee. The campus center is just a minute away from here. Maybe we could talk there?" Before Ben could respond, Elena was already briskly walking down the hall, and she made it just in time to enter the elevator after Alicia. While the elevator made its rocky way down to the ground floor, Elena silently hope that she was right in her assessment that Ben wouldn't try anything in front of a witness.

The campus was quiet, but there were enough students being let out of class for Elena to remain in someone's line of sight all the way to the campus center. This whole way she was playing through escape scenarios in her mind. Did Ben have his hands in the pocket of his overcoat because he was cold, or was he holding something? What would he do if she just took off? How would he try to isolate her once in the campus center? After all, it wouldn't be especially busy right now…Would it raise suspicion to try to get him to go somewhere else? And where?… Amazingly, while running through these scenarios in her head, Elena managed to keep up a conversation with Ben. Maybe it was all her practice describing her research to colleagues while mentally reviewing their scholarly profiles and the likelihood of a new hire being announced in their departments. However she managed it, Ben seemed completely unaware of what she was thinking.

When they stepped into the campus center, Elena was dismayed to see that the cafe had already closed and the building was nearly empty. Ben was trying to guide her deeper in to the building's recesses when Elena noticed that Sasha was still sitting in the closed cafe, doing homework.

"Oh my God!" Elena exclaimed. "I'm so sorry to do this to you again, but I forgot that I have another meeting with a student scheduled for right now. She's been waiting for me at the cafe. I—"
Ben grabbed her arm and pressed something into her side. "Don't scream," he whispered. "You've already taken up most of my day. I'm getting tired of it. Let's go down this way so I can do my job." He started leading her toward an empty hallway.

"Professor Malatesta!" Suddenly, Elena heard Sasha call out behind her. "Professor Malatesta! Did you forget about our meeting? I've been waiting here for the past half hour."

Elena and the man turned around together. "Of course, I didn't forget. I just wanted to say a quick word to my colleague here, but we're finished now. I'm at your disposal." She could feel the pressure release on her side as she said this.

"So who was that guy?" Sasha asked once they were out of earshot. "I hope you don't mind me intruding…It seemed like you wanted an excuse not to talk to him."

"He was just—" Elena didn't want to involve Sasha in this situation any more than she needed to. "Like I said, he's just a colleague," was the best cover she could think of. And then she added in a very different tone of voice: "Thank you."

As it turned out, Sasha actually did want to speak to Elena. She had spent the last week researching an article on the Murray Otis lecture for the student newspaper, *The Interrogator*. So far, the information that she had found didn't quite add up, and she was hoping that a faculty member might be able to give her a little more perspective about what was going on. Since Elena was in a hurry to get away from campus, Sasha asked her questions on the way to Elena's car.

"Oh, I'm sorry, but I have no idea about this lecture," Elena told her. "I think a student group invited him."

"That's exactly the thing I don't get. Who invited him? The Young Aristotelian Society has voiced support for the lecture, but they deny that they were the ones to invite Otis. So, I asked around at other student organizations and everyone denies inviting him. But here's where it gets weird: the posters say the event is sponsored by something called the Institute for a Better Society. I tried looking them up, but they don't seem to exist. I mean, they do have a website, but I can't find any record of them sponsoring events anywhere else. There's no answer at the phone number listed on their website. Isn't that weird?"

"Yeah, it is," Elena agreed. It actually didn't sound that strange to her— she pretty much assumed every controversial decision at the College was made in whispers under the cover of shadows and all witnesses were promptly disposed of. But she was also only half-listening because she was still much more concerned with figuring out what this "Ben" was after. Feeling guilty for not paying more attention, she did what she always did when she zoned out during a conversation with a student—she asked an open-ended question: "Do you know who runs it?"

"The Institute? Malcolm Hailey. That's the president's name. But if you search it online, you just get some dead British baron. There's no current information. The only person I could find anything on was the vice president: an alum of Bellwether, some kind of consultant…"

"I guess he wanted to have an impact at his alma mater," Elena felt good that she was contributing to the conversation again. Now she asked the question she probably should have posed before: "So what does this group stand for?"

"That's the other thing. I can't tell. Every single page is just incoherent nonsense about 'wanting to protect our nations priorities' or 'fighting for a fairer world for our youth.' There aren't any firm policy positions anywhere on the website…. Actually though, going back to the vice president, he's a consultant at a firm called Moahil Loch."

"Moahil Loch?" Elena repeated.

"You've heard of them?"

"Yeah, they've been working with the administration here on balancing the College's budget."

"Can you tell me anything else about them?"

"I'm really sorry, Sasha," Elena said. At this point, she felt a need to come clean about the fact that she couldn't focus on anything Sasha was saying. "This sounds like a fascinating investigative article, but it's been a very long day, and I think it would be better to go into this another time. Maybe we could touch base about it tomorrow? Are you free at 11?"

"Sure."

"Okay, great. I'll see you in my office then!"

The first thing Elena did when she got in her car was look up the address of the nearest police station. She wasn't going to try to explain things to campus security again. In fact, she didn't trust them after her last experience. How had the Owl known she would be walking down that road? If someone was specifically targeting her and the other part-time faculty, they must have known who she was. How else could they have found it out? No, she would go to the real police and file a report… Hm. A report… Well, that might be a problem. What the hell would she say? She couldn't mention the owl mask—being stalked by a school mascot didn't sound especially serious. Would it get Cristina in trouble to mention the warnings she gave her? Actually, the more important question was whether anyone would believe she gave them. After all, it definitely *sounded* a little paranoid to say one's Department Manager had repeatedly tried to pass her discreet warnings in between her normal departmental functions—plus, she hadn't even retained the post-it note (compelling evidence as it was). She definitely couldn't mention her whole suspicion about the brainwashing at Wanesdale. For one thing, it would definitely make her sound crazy right off the bat. (And for another, even though Connie hadn't said anything, Elena could see how retelling her encounter with "Amrita" at the cafe could sound a little racist. It definitely didn't help that, besides Connie, all of her friends were White… Really, this wasn't the time to think about that though.) So, she could tell the police about a missed call, a bloody stuffed animal, and the fact that a representative from a study abroad program was very insistent about talking to her... And now she was turning the car around.

Her next thought was to go to Connie. After all, Elena listened to Connie's crazy shit all the time, so the least Connie could do was put up with Elena a little longer today—and who knew, maybe she would even be helpful for once. But then again, Connie didn't seem to have a lot of patience left the last time she talked to her. In fact, the very act of imagining how she would explain to Connie what just happened at Bellwether made Elena suddenly start to doubt her own sanity once more. No, she thought while pulling into a gas station, I need to figure out what to do on my own.

While refueling her tank, Elena could only confirm that she was incapable of thinking straight at the moment and that she really wanted to be home. When she arrived at her apartment minutes later, she was so distracted that she didn't even notice how easily the door opened, as if someone had broken the lock, and she had already dropped her bag on the counter and started to walk to the fridge for some filtered water when she noticed someone sitting perfectly still in the chair next to her desk.

Her visitor wore all black and had the head of a giant barn owl.

CHAPTER SEVENTEEN

Minerva the Owl had become the official mascot of Bellwether College only recently. For most of the College's history, its sports teams didn't have an official mascot. It was only in the late 1950s that a group of alumni began to draw attention to a lack of unifying tradition and advocated for a new mascot reflecting the College's "true" character. They settled on the institution's namesake, James T. Bellwether, a local mayor, philanthropist, and military officer. For the first two decades of this mascot's existence, the new tradition was represented primarily by a single male student in a wig and colonial garb, whose performance at sporting events was invariably bolstered by a heavy-drinking coterie in college sweaters who would loudly cheer him on. In 1981, the mascot received its first major change, as the Class of 1950 pooled money to buy a giant foam head and hands for the performer to wear. This reinvigorated the tradition, and for a while Bellwether was often seen on campus, pepping up the sports teams before big events, leading a marching band up and down campus during Reading Period, and directing a chorus in singing the newly rediscovered "Ballad of our Benefactor," a nineteenth-century ode to Bellwether, with the chorus: "Bellwether, our cap's feather,/to our school's pride we're true/to the father of our Alma Mater/until our days be through."

Despite a dedicated following, however, Bellwether was not widely popular on campus. This partly had to do with such benign factors as the general low attendance at College sporting events and the intrinsic silliness of this big-foam-headed man. But the main source of controversy was a fact well known at the time of the mascot's selection and restated every several years by student columnists in the *Interrogator*. The issue had to do with certain views that were expressed in unambiguous terms in Bellwether's letters and that appear to have been guiding principles for his actions as mayor. It makes little sense to rehash the matter here. Suffice to say, the campus community was divided into two camps—a rabid group of defenders of the newly traditional practice of celebrating Bellwether as a College icon and an ever-increasing body of students who felt marginalized by the celebration of this figure—with a substantial buffer of the apathetic preventing direct conflict most of the time. This situation had come to a head only seven years ago, during a year of mass protests on campus, when the anti-Bellwether camp finally succeeded in forcing a referendum on the College mascot. Critics might dismiss this referendum as a means of distracting from the students' more structural criticisms of the College by focusing on an entirely symbolic matter, while also eliminating a mascot that was starting to attract unwelcome criticism in the national press. Be that as it may, however, Bellwether's days were finally numbered.

The search for a replacement might have been difficult in view of the general dearth of adequate imagery associated with the College. No one seemed to understand why there was an ouroboros on the school's seal, and this image presented practical difficulties for a costume designer. The College's only notable alum was Pete Rossetano, a confidence man who had amassed quite a fortune before being shot in a bar fight. The College actually had no official colors, as a kind of homage to the daltonism from which Bellwether famously suffered. Even the local wildlife was disappointing, consisting mainly of various rodents and deer that would hardly be effective for rallying morale. In short, the situation might have been desperate had a group of alumni not offered a clear consensus candidate: Minerva, the barn owl.

This mascot also traced its origins back to a figure from the College's past, but one who led a much more quiet life than Bellwether (as long as certain unsubstantiated rumors were ignored). This individual was David Leland Howlsley III, who served the College as a Professor of Religion from 1880-1892 before becoming its ninth president. Very little was known about Howlsley, except that he was an efficient administrator and students remember him to be an inspired lecturer. As part of his studies, he had amassed an impressive collection of rare books related to medieval Christian thought, which were now housed in a special collection at the Ercoli Library. Along with his book collection, a massive portrait of Howlsley had been donated to the library, and it hung over the entryway since then. This portrait showed Howlsley to be an imposing figure with a sharp nose, bushy white eyebrows, and an angular forehead. Yet, most library patrons hardly noticed Howlsley's stern eyes staring at them, for their attention was immediately drawn to the focal point of the portrait: Howlsley's massive pet barn owl, Minerva. It appeared as though by some bizarre whim either the artist or the sitter had come to the strange decision that the owl should be painted at nearly twice its actual size, such that it was roughly as large as a medium-sized dog. No one knew why this was case, but the picture was widely beloved by students. What's more, an alumna sculptor was so taken with the painting that she created a three-dimensional Minerva that was installed in front of the college store.

In short, this owl was already becoming a widely recognized unofficial symbol of the college among students and alumni, and it only took the push of this referendum to make it official. Within a year, the college store was stocked with Minerva t-shirts, sweatshirts, coffee mugs, etc.—including adorable little stuffed owls. The official Minerva mascot costume took a little longer, mainly because the first mask made for it turned out to be the head of a great horned owl, rather than a barn owl. Once they had this ornithological confusion worked out, however, the costume was a major improvement over Bellwether's leering mug in terms of both historical connotations and its likelihood of scaring innocent children in the crowd.

Now that Elena stood face to face with the Owl, she could see that her initial assessment was a little off. For one thing, he (the Owl continued to read as a *he*, even though Elena had no definitive evidence of "his" gender) was not as tall and slender as she had remembered him. In fact, he stood before her somewhat awkwardly, stooped over a little bit. Up close, the mask looked surprisingly tattered and gave off a musty odor. She hadn't ever actually been to an athletics event at Bellwether, so she couldn't say for certain whether this was the mask used for games, but it looked like it had spent a long time, maybe even over a decade, in storage. She was most struck by the eyes. Even though she knew the person inside must be looking through the mouth, Elena stared at the Owl's dead, oversized eyes with a completely paralyzing sense of terror.

The Owl moved toward her, with the awkward, lumbering gait of a serial killer in a slasher film. She watched him and internally, screamed, *"Get the hell out!"* But she was completely unable to move. When he had moved within striking distance of the paralyzed Elena—

He handed her a typed note.

"You must excuse my appearance," it read. Although it was typed in large font, it was a little difficult to read. The printer must have been running out of toner. "I must disguise my identity to protect my own safety. (The form of my visage is a matter of convenience—there are a surprising number of owl masks in storage behind the athletic facilities.) Do not try to speak to me—I will not answer questions. Give me your car keys and I will lead you to what you need to know."

In the vast majority of cases, the decision to hand one's keys over to a masked stranger is not made willingly. Today, however, was precisely the type of day on which one makes atypical decisions, and there was something hypnotizing about staring into those sewn dead eyes. Elena found herself reasoning in a most peculiar manner, as if she was trying to find an excuse to trust this peculiar being. After all, if the Owl was a deranged killer, he was evidently very roundabout in his ways and there would probably be an opportunity to escape later—and at this point, this thought was actually fairly comforting. Elena was also curious how the Owl would fit into her Civic and drive with that giant foam head—maybe he would take it off, and she would find out who was behind the mask? But more than anything, Elena was curious. And if pursuing a graduate degree in the humanities signaled anything about her character, it was that she had a tendency to let curiosity outweigh her common sense. So, with an absolutely unjustified feeling of confidence, she handed over her keys.

The Owl immediately returned her keys, along with a hospital bracelet and another note:

"Obviously I cannot drive wearing this mask. It was a test to see if you trust me. Glad to see that you do. Now, here is address for you to go to: 237 Prospect Pike, in Hatchers Hole. Put on the bracelet as well. You should go in through the service entrance in back. Be discreet. If anyone catches you, act very confused and stumble a little bit. If they ask what you're doing, say you are **awaiting reassignment**. Remember this phrase. Do everything they say. Make no sudden movements. But be sure to run before they secure the clamps. You'll know when."

You'll know when?! What the hell kind of advice was that? Also, 'before they secure the clamps' sounds very late to run. It would seem far better to get away before the clamps come out, or even before clamps have become a consideration. Presumably, the Owl was trying to warn her of the fact that they clamp people down on the other side of this service entrance, but this just kinda seemed like a dickish way to put it—like he was trying to be clever or something. She didn't feel like the Owl had really though much about her position in all this, and that was kinda irritating. Nonetheless, she decided to abide by the "no questions" rule. She was clearly living in a world she didn't understand, and breaking the few rules that she had been given seemed like tempting fate.

After a pause, the Owl took out another note, quickly drew a couple lines on it, and handed it to her:

"You probably wonder why—considering my desire for anonymity—I came in person to deliver you this address. The answer is simple: I had to be sure that you would go. It was only by seeing you in person that I could assess whether you were likely to go on this mission." The next sentence was crossed out and the following underlined: "~~Now, I can clearly see I've been disappointed.~~ As expected, you have convinced me to trust in you to investigate further."

Elena thought this last note was especially irritating. Yes, he had correctly inferred that she was planning to investigate the address he'd given her, but as far as she was concerned he had no reason to feel so confident of his success. How did he know she wasn't just pretending to play along to get rid of him? More generally, she would like to see more acknowledgement from the Owl that arriving at her house dressed as an owl was a *bad plan*. Elena felt sure that a less tired, frustrated, and confused person wouldn't have been quite so receptive to the message being delivered in this format. He was damn lucky she had taught two classes today.

There ensued another silence, lasting several minutes this time. Finally, the Owl handed Elena another pre-typed note. This one said, simply:

"Please go now. I will see myself out."

The Owl sat back down in Elena's chair with his hands on his knees, staring at the wall. Not really sure what else to do, Elena left him sitting in her apartment.

CHAPTER EIGHTEEN

While driving to the address provided by the Owl, Elena tried to remember what Vladimir Propp had said about the role of animals in a folk tale. Perhaps this wasn't the best moment to contemplate formalist theories of narrative—or maybe this was the exact right moment to be thinking about narrative logic, since real world logic didn't seem to be functioning anymore.

Her actions so far had been determined by the assumption that she was the hero and the Owl was some kind of magical helper, whose role was to give her something that she needed to complete her journey (the address). His role must be that of a magical agent in Elena's quest, and the address that he had given her would somehow enable her to solve whatever was happening at Bellwether... Or maybe not. After all, if he was leading her to her death, that would also be advancing the narrative. Was there any hard and fast rule prohibiting the villain from appearing in the guise of an animal helper? What if he was leading her into some kind of elaborate trap? Did Propp ever talk about how the hero is to know whether it's a real helper or a trick? Probably not. That's the problem with formalism, really: it doesn't offer a lot of useful advice for anyone but the writer. If you find yourself living inside the story, then you're pretty much screwed. So really, she shouldn't be taking it so seriously. This was an im-Propp-er use narrative theory. Ha. (Was that funny? Or was she just really tired?) Maybe she should try the "im-Propp-er" joke on Connie later, or what if she said something about Propping up—oh shit! need not to swerve like that. Need to focus on driving! God, she really was tired... Teaching two classes was exhausting on days she wasn't being stalked! Maybe she should just go to the cops? Nah, she was pretty much there already, so it was really too late to be thinking of alternatives. In fact,—son of a—there it goes on the other side of the street. Okay, she could just do a U-turn (or really a P-turn) at the next jug handle. No one ever has to drive anywhere in folk tales, though, she figured, this would all be harder on horseback. Anyway, here we go, just ease around the turn back onto the highway. And here we go— pulling into the parking lot. Wow, she was very nervous about this. She would need to calm down a little before going inside...

The building didn't look especially ominous from the outside. It looked like it could belong to a dentist or a tax accounting firm or pretty much any business that needed to rent a couple offices. Then again, Elena had seen plenty of movies where nondescript buildings turn out to contain nightmares. As Elena pulled into the parking lot behind the building, she saw that there was indeed a small loading dock, and the door was wide open as promised. Obviously, the Owl must work in some capacity with whoever rented this building and knew how cavalier they were with their security. Elena parked her car next to the two other cars in the lot. She took a few deep breaths to calm down before continuing.

Sasha had once remarked that Italian thrillers would be much shorter if either ordinary people made better decisions or the police spent less time taking smoke breaks... These movies always seemed to star some reporter or other person with zero crime-fighting experience who decided to get to the bottom of things when the police proved feckless. This person would always put themselves in danger to gather evidence that would turn out to be misleading, and the truth of the matter would only reveal itself when the amateur investigator was in mortal danger—not only that, but it would also prove to be something infuriatingly impossible to guess from the gathered evidence...

The loading dock was empty. Elena crept up a ramp leading to a white door. She slowly, carefully pushed the door open and saw—a tidy, white-walled hallway reminiscent of her optometrist's office.

The building seemed empty. She walked down a long hallway, trying doors as she went. The first one she opened was a private bathroom, and the next led to a closet, which was filled with green tunics for some unknown reason. (To Elena they looked like graduation robes redesigned as sexy Halloween costumes.) A little further down, she found a room that looked like some kind of a doctor's office. It was sparsely furnished: in the corner opposite the door, there was an examination chair with a long metal table next to it, and along the wall nearest the door, there was a two-tiered cabinet with a workspace atop the bottom tier. Elena went to examine the papers in this workspace. Most of these were more or less incomprehensible, containing geometric shapes accompanied by unfamiliar symbols. Then, Elena noticed a clipboard with a list of names. She didn't recognize the list at first, but then she noticed Sandra's name, and a little higher on the page there was Amrita (she must have gone right past it). Each name had some words scribbled next to it in a column labeled

"Evaluation." It was difficult to read the handwriting, but Elena could just barely make out the words "satisfactory" next to Amrita and "needs improvement" next to Sandra. When she looked at the list more closely, suddenly she recognized about two-thirds of the names as faculty at Bellwether—all teaching in the Modern Languages Department. The sheet was labeled "Reassigned Faculty Initial Status Report." Lastly, Elena noticed that one name was scratched out with a little sticky note attached to the paper next to it. "Damaged during extraction," it said in a more legible hand. "Irreparable." Although Elena couldn't make out the name that was scratched out, she could see that it was right between Erica Nyman and Darren Oppenheimer. Making a quick inference, she dropped the list in fear and fled the room.

At this point, if Elena were watching her own actions in a movie, she would known exactly what she should do next: Run. Get in her car and get as far away from this facility as possible. Nothing good could come from remaining there. But living through this situation, she read it differently. She was slower to acknowledge that there was any real danger. Her suspicions seemed so outlandish that she could only half believe them—in fact, the whole chain of events where a strange stalker kept approaching her in-between her regular class schedule and arguments with Connie seemed so bizarre that it was hard to credit any of it as a real threat—at least not to her personally. She was starting to have real concerns about what may have occurred to the other faculty in her department, but it was almost impossible to believe that she personally could be threatened by a situation so manifestly absurd.

So she kept exploring.

The next open room she came to was some kind of office. Along the righthand wall there stood a midsize wardrobe, the door to which was locked. Opposite the wardrobe was a large wooden desk. In the corner by the window, there was a tall, locked cabinet full of various knickknacks. Elena wasn't entirely sure what they were, but they reminded her of the kinds of things one of her great aunts would collect: a miscellany of religious artifacts (prayer candles, saint's relics, etc.) and gaudy baubles (such as decorated plates and fancy perfume bottles). Interspersed throughout the room she noted a surprising amount of Bellwether merchandise: a lanyard hanging from a desk-drawer knob, an owl mug on the desk, a couple stuffed owls tossed in the corner…

There was a stack of papers on the desk filled with various tables and graphs. While some of them looked medical, others looked more related to finances. Above the desk, there was a small bookshelf that included *Navigating Academia, Improve Your Casting in Five Minutes a Day, Consulting for Beginners, Stop Stallin' and Start Stalin: How to Become a Leader in Your Business, Caudex Maleficorum,* and a bound master's thesis by someone named

Santiago Aguilar titled *Tenure-Bound: Understanding Academic Culture Through Sacher-Masoch*. In the upper desk drawer, Elena found a variety of shaving implements, carefully arranged. The middle drawer contained a collection of brochures from International Horizons, detailing their supposed programs in Paris, Berlin, Tokyo, Barcelona, and Rome. The lower desk drawer contained a portfolio of documents: when Elena flipped through it she found research and promotional materials apparently prepared by Moahil Loch for Bellwether College. The document that caught her attention was labeled "On the Reallocation of Intellectual Resources," and it outlined with copious graphs and data the economic benefit of "reallocating resources" from the humanities to the business school and the hard sciences. She read a paragraph of the text:

"Moahil Loch advisers can help you effectively shift your resources from your poorly functioning departments to those that contribute more to your institution's well-being. For many administrators the main obstacle to accomplishing this task is simply fear of change. Even when they know what course of action will benefit the academic community, they sometimes cleave to outdated values or concerns that certain individuals may be adversely affected. Our advisers will help you to allay these fears and we will simplify the staffing issues that inevitably come up as a result of making such a significant step forward."

Could this be it? Was that what this place was for? Was it possible that the consulting firm brought the faculty members they intended to lay off here for some kind of compulsory retraining? Elena had read articles about how overspecialized academic training had become, and how difficult it was to fit academics with new jobs outside their area of expertise. If a corporation could come up with a "flash retraining" method that instantly converted these capable, intelligent individuals into specialists in something more economically viable, that would be an earth-shattering intervention. It might even save higher education. So, it was just possible that this location was a kind of testing facility for this type of training. It was just possible that the humanities faculty at Bellwether were being abducted as guinea pigs for this experiment. If only she could be sure...

Elena's thoughts were broken off by the sound of footsteps coming down the hall. With a heavy feeling of terror, she realized that she had failed to close the door behind her when entering this room. She hurried over to the door, but the footsteps were already coming close—she couldn't slam it shut without revealing she was inside. Out of options, she decided to hide on the other side of the open door, hoping the footsteps would just continue down the hall.

They didn't.

A few moments later, Elena could hear someone stop in the hallway and walk into the room. This person stood there for a moment, likely examining the room, and then—seemed satisfied with what they saw. Elena held back a sigh of relief as she heard footsteps retreating back toward the hall and watched the door start to swing shut. It looked like maybe she would escape undetected after all... But then she heard the most terrifying sound she had ever heard in her life.

It was Rihanna.

Connie was calling her cellphone.

CHAPTER NINETEEN

When her hiding place suddenly swung away, Elena was exposed to the gaze of a deliberate, clinical-looking man, whose single black stud earring was not enough to add character to his bland appearance. Even at these close quarters, his rather generic face seemed to disappear behind his glasses.

At this point, Elena felt she had little choice but to continue placing her trust in the Owl's advice. She blinked a few times as if confused and started to shamble further into the corner. Wishing she had got more direction, she bumped up against the wall several times, like a wind-up toy directed by an unkind child, hamming up her stumbling all the while to make sure it would be noticed.

"Stop!" the man called out.

She complied.

The man walked over and checked her bracelet. He turned her around to examine her better. Looking at the brightly colored collar and tie under his white lab coat, Elena thought again about how hard he was trying to make himself seem interesting. In her opinion, these efforts only undermined the one thing he had going for him—his total seriousness. As things stood, he looked more like an actor dressed up as a scientist than an actual lab technician. She tried not to get distracted and pretended not to notice as he took the still-ringing cellphone from her hand.

"What are you doing here?" he asked.

"Awaiting reassignment." In Elena's head, her voice sounded unconvincing—like she was doing a bad impression of a robot from a scifi movie. But the man didn't seem suspicious at all. If anything, he appeared vaguely annoyed.

"Hm. Awaiting reassignment... How long have you been here?—No. Don't answer that. I hate listening to one of you talk at this stage. It's all preprogrammed phrases and incoherent nonsense." He seemed to be caught up on this last thought, adding to himself in a low voice: "Santiago might have come up with this process, but his work's just so crude. In the end, he just creates mindless zombies. But *we* engineer the souls for them… Or really, *I* do and Dana sometimes helps…" At this point, he seemed to remember that the woman was standing there and addressed her: "Now come along. Follow me down the hall."

Elena's first instinct was simply to run away the moment she stepped out into the hall. But she was also curious to find out more about this place, and this guy sounded like a talker. Besides, there was now a woman coming down the hall behind her (perhaps, "Dana"), and she didn't know what these people were capable of doing or how many more people might be in the hall. So she decided it might be safer to wait for a clear opening.

This newcomer quickly caught up with them and helped escort Elena to the doctor's office where she had been before. "Where did you find her?" she asked. "I thought we were done for the night."

"She was in Santiago's office," the man responded. "He must have left the door open, and she just stumbled in."

"Again? Christ…Why doesn't he just use restraints in the recovery room? It seems like one in four of them have been walkers lately."

(Did she really just say "walkers"? Elena thought. There couldn't really exist people who talked like that, could there?)

"He considers it an unnecessary risk," the man explained from the corner. He returned carrying the clipboard Elena had seen earlier. "He believes—with no real evidence, as far as I'm concerned—that restraining a patient immediately following an operation would frighten the patient too soon after the realignment, ingraining a fear response in the patient's new thought patterns, which might ultimately lead to complications down the line. Honestly, I believe he anthropomorphizes these creatures too much— who's to say that they would react to the restraints with fear? They seem perfectly docile when we tie them down for Stage Two, and sometimes that's just half-an-hour later. Besides, the whole point is that they aren't very human when he's done with them, so they don't react the way we do."

"Yeah, I know all that," the woman said. "By 'why doesn't he just restrain them,' I really just meant, 'he should go ahead and restrain them.' But thanks for the explanation."

"Well, I found this on her," the man said, holding up Elena's phone.

"Again?"

"Yep," he said, placing Elena's phone on the cabinet. "It's a little sad how whenever they get a call or message they seem to want to walk around. It's as if they have some vague memory of noise from their devices being a signal they need to do something—it appears that this type of habit is more persistent than most parts of their identities."

"Humans are pretty dumb," the woman offered.

The man was now staring at Elena. In an odd way, his stare reminded her of that Ben guy who had tried to corner her at Bellwether—it felt like this man, too, was looking past her. "Give me your first and last names," he ordered. Once she had responded, he began looking through a list on his clipboard. He evidently couldn't find what he was looking for, since he asked for her name again. Irritated, he shoved the clipboard into other woman's hands and left the room.

Unlike the man, this woman didn't stare past Elena but tried not to look in her direction at all, training her focus on the clipboard. Looking at her, Elena wondered how she had become involved in this whole abduction and nonconsensual surgery thing. The other guy looked like a faceless technical type, someone who would be a good hire for any boss planning to commit war crimes. But this young woman seemed much more, Elena didn't know, relatable. She had cool green hair, eyebrow piercings, and low voice that sounded both no nonsense and relaxed. Back when she was in high school, Elena imagined having a friend like this in college—this girl was pretty much exactly teenage Elena's idea of a cool young adult. Maybe if things went wrong at some point, she could try reasoning with her. Who knows? Maybe she would help Elena survive and they would eventually become friends!.. On the other hand, she might want to find out a little more about her first. After all, she was evidently involved in what appeared to be some kind of odd brainwashing project.

"Okay, here she is. Still on the pick-up list. It would appear that Ben once again neglected to do the paperwork at drop-off. See here? She was scheduled for earlier today, then he pushed it back. He must have finally got her late this afternoon and decided not to bother with the paperwork before going home."

"Why does Ben get to rush home? We've had to stay here every evening this week."

"Come on, Dana. You know we can't exactly unionize. Besides, the work schedule obviously won't matter after tomorrow."

"Well, Ben should watch out," Dana responded. "He might not still be around tomorrow. Between losing that guy yesterday and running late on this delivery..."

"Still, it's strange that Ben didn't update the lists. Maybe I should call him to confirm?"

"C'mon, Simon." (Oh, that was his name!) "I just want to get out of here. She's here, she's tagged, and she's obviously a vegetable. So go get your little tablet and your brain wand, and we'll have her up and running again in no time!"

"Fine," Simon said gruffly, leaving the room. "I'll be right back with the stuff. Take care of the clamps in the meantime."

At the word "clamps," Elena acknowledged that her hopes of befriending Dana were likely naive. It was time to run like hell. So, when Dana crouched down to take something out of the cabinet, Elena jetted for the door, knocking Dana's head against the cabinet in the process. She heard a sound behind her that was likely Simon chasing her down the hall, but she sprinted back to the loading dock and made it out into the parking lot without seeing anyone else. As she was driving away, Simon tried to run in front of her car to force her to stop, but he seemed to chicken out at the last minute, only making it as far as her right headlight. She easily swerved around him and drove out of the parking lot.

When Elena made it home, she found her door unlocked. Of course, she thought, the stupid Owl didn't bother locking the door. She couldn't really be too surprised that her home intruder lacked a basic sense of courtesy. And how much would it cost to get a stronger lock? Did the Owl even think about things like this before he decided to break in? Maybe Elena liked living in the false security of thinking her home was perfectly safe from intruders without shelling out more money and getting into a fight with her landlord...

If she had been thinking more clearly, Elena might not have gone into the apartment right then. She might have decided to go anywhere but into the one, unprotected place where people knew she could be found. But it was late, she was tired, she still didn't understand anything she had just seen—and most of all, she wanted to be home. And so she swung the door open and stepped into her apartment, where once again someone was sitting in the dark, waiting for her. This time it wasn't the Owl but a woman who had evidently been crying and was now literally shaking with agitation.

It was Connie.

CHAPTER TWENTY

"You're such an asshole!"

This is the first thing Connie said when Elena walked in the door. Now she was staring at Elena with a concentrated anger that she had rarely seen.

"You're an asshole, El. You don't answer my calls or texts, you leave the door to your apartment unlocked—even cracked open, just inviting people to come inside—you're not here, so that anything could have happened—and all this is after coming to Wanesdale with that crazy story about something happening to your coworkers. And…and…Goddamn it! Why didn't you answer your phone?"

"Connie, listen I've just seen some crazy things."

"No, listen. I need to tell you something—" "No you don't understand—" "*You* don't understand—" "Connie, please—" "Elena, this is really imp—" "Connie, we have to go." "We—" "WE HAVE TO GO" "—what?" "LET'S GET IN YOUR CAR NOW!"

After a brief argument, Connie and Elena drove off in the former's car. It was Elena's idea to leave her own car behind, just in case Dana had recorded her license plate number as she was swerving around Simon. Elena didn't understand what was going on, or how her name had got onto some mad scientists' abduction list, but they were sure as hell not going to find her sitting in her own goddamn apartment waiting for them.

When they arrived at Connie's apartment, Elena spent twenty minutes trying to explain everything that happened, or at least, what she understood of it. Initially, she planned to keep the Owl part secret, since that seemed like the part that would be hardest to credit, but somehow she ended up leaving even this in. The main difficulty was trying to define what they were doing in the lab. She figured it was some kind of brainwashing, but that sounded a little silly to say, so she very much wished that she had a better sense of what kind of neurological surgery was being done. If she had been paying more attention to her friend, however, she would have noticed that Connie actually didn't seem especially shocked or incredulous about anything Elena was telling her—really, she just looked deeply annoyed.

"Are you done?" Connie asked finally. "First, let me just say that you're an idiot for investigating that place on your own... You should have called me... And you're also incredibly self-centered. All this time, did you even wonder *why* I was sitting here listening to all this? Most people would have cut you off at Owl man passing notes—if not much earlier—and *especially* after what I saw earlier today with that girl at the cafeteria. But I didn't. Do you know why that is? Do you know why I was so quick to jump in the car when you said we had to leave your apartment? Do you have any idea?"

Elena had to admit that she didn't have any idea.

"Well, let me explain." Here Connie paused for a minute because she realized that it was actually a rather difficult thing to explain. When she resumed, her tone was somewhat softened. "Look. I saw Sandra too. *Your* Sandra, the one from your department. I saw her at Wanesdale, and it was obvious that something was really wrong."

"Was she teaching a biology class?"

"No. Or at least, not at the moment I saw her. Actually, I should explain that she wasn't the first one I saw... Just listen. I was down by the library, and I thought I saw that Portuguese girl from your department—the weird one who always talks to me when I stop by? I usually try to avoid her, but it seemed like we made eye contact, and you know how I abide by the eye contact rule, so I went over to say 'hi.' But it was like she didn't recognize me. And the really weird thing was that she was acting normal, or like normal for other people, just giving short responses and trying to get away. It was also kinda odd that she wouldn't tell me why she was on our campus—it sounded like she was teaching something there, but I couldn't get a clear response on what, or when she had started. Then, after a few minutes she abruptly just kinda walked off mid-conversation. So all this was unusual, and naturally I remembered your little freak out earlier, so I just sorta decided to follow her. To see what she was doing at Wanesdale. And it was easy to do because she wasn't paying any attention to me—once she had walked by me, it was like she forgot I existed. So I followed her into the Life Sciences building. It was late already, and the building was pretty empty. She went down to the basement level, past some classrooms and offices to this room marked 'Adjunct Office.' There were like six people sitting in there, including her, completely silent, none of them looking at each other. And it's not like they were all doing work. They were just sitting silently, and really straight in their chairs, and staring off into space. I don't know who all of them were, but I recognized a couple of them from your Department. There was one woman who looked just like Katie, except with kinda, I don't know, deader eyes. And that young Spanish instructor, the one who's still in grad school, but he looked a lot older, at least around the eyes... I don't know how to describe it, but it was incredibly creepy. I mean, I was standing in the doorway for maybe five minutes and no one looked up at me. No one even moved during that time. Not at all. Then, I heard someone coming down the hall. At this point, I was pretty creeped out, so I kinda tried to hide behind one of those big archways they have for the fire doors, but there wasn't really a good place for it. I watched this person approach, and when they got close I suddenly realized it was Sandra. I was relieved. Maybe she could tell me what was going on, or even if she couldn't, it was good just to see another normal person. So I walk up to her. And she just stops the moment she sees me and lets out a loud scream. Not like, I don't know, a shout of surprise. A weird, unbroken scream. It didn't seem natural. And everyone back in the office starts screaming in response. In the same unnatural way. Suddenly, I can hear someone else coming down the stairs, running this time, and I push past Sandra to hide in one of the bathrooms. As soon as the footsteps run by me to the adjunct room, I run the hell out of there and start driving." She added accusingly: "That's also when I started calling you, by the way..."

"Look, I told you why I didn't answer my phone. Those assholes took it from me."

"Well, anyway—who do you think they are?"

"I don't know. They seem to be some kind of scientists. I was thinking that maybe they were hired by a corporation to perform experiments on educators. Like a kind of rapid retraining to transfer instructors from one subject to another. They could be—I don't know, this is just a guess—doing some kind of brain surgery to retrain language instructors in more profitable subjects, like engineering or finance."

"That doesn't make any sense."

"Well, I'm not sure exactly how they were converting people. I guess it could be hypnotism instead of surgery. Or—who knows?"

"No, it's not that. I'm fine with the brainwashing part. There's probably someone out there who knows how to do that. It's the economics that don't make any sense. Think about it. How much money could they possibly make with a bunch of zombie teachers? Adjunct salaries are pretty minuscule, so how would they end up saving any money by doing this, especially when they need to pay for weird neurological manipulation?"

"Well,"—Elena had a tendency to get defensive when she thought her ideas were being dismissed out of hand—"I think a lot of science positions involve teaching more sessions per week than most humanities classes. And of course, grad students in the sciences have a lot more professional opportunities after graduation—"

"Yeah, no. When Wanesdale is understaffed, they usually just get some of their most advanced undergrads to help with TA duties in the introductory classes. It costs next to nothing, especially compared to some scientific procedure and whatever it costs to feed and upkeep these zombie teachers, or whatever you'd call them. Also, there's the risk of getting caught. Regardless of the details, it would be really bad for everyone involved to be caught kidnapping and brainwashing people. And they must have taken at least eight different people—if they keep up this rate, people will definitely notice."

"Apparently, it's not something they're worried about. That building didn't seem to have a lot of security."

"Doesn't that seem weird to you?"

"Well, yeah. But what do you think it is?"

"Who knows? It has to be something they don't plan to keep secret for long. Which, if movies can be trusted, must mean that they expect it will be too late by the time people figure it out. Whatever they're planning, it's big—and it's happening soon... Do you think they could be terrorists?"

"Terrorist consultants? Using zombies to pull off some kind of what—a bombing at Wanesdale? Sounds far-fetched."

"Is it though?"—Connie also got defensive when she felt her ideas were being dismissed—"After all, one might argue that the outbreak of terroristic acts worldwide is a logical consequence of neoliberal world order, which includes the zombification of the labor force. Thus, the violence of this terrorist act would be legible as a manifestation of the dissonance between one's internally cultivated personal identity and one's externally determined value in the workforce—between the given individual's agentive and instrumental functions within the political economy."

"No, I'm pretty sure it's not that."

"Okay, so what do you have?"

"Maybe they are testing a new mind control technique for the government? Did you read that goat book a few years back? The government does some shady things..."

"I don't see how that negates my hypothesis. State-sponsored terrorism—"

"It doesn't matter! We need to go to the police."

"Do you really think the police will take us seriously? You couldn't even get campus security to investigate. We need some kind of documentation. We need to go back to that building with cameras and tape recorders."

"You mean your phone, right?"

"Yeah." Connie stopped, suddenly preoccupied with something. "So...*your* phone. You said they took it?"

"Yeah. Right when they caught me."

"So they have access to your contacts?"

"I guess so. But they won't be able to unlock it, right?"

"Elena..." Connie stared at her for a second. "I called you." She waited again to see if Elena was grasping the gravity of this statement. "They don't need to unlock it to see that. It would just pop up on the screen." She sat for a moment staring at the ground. "How is my name entered in your caller ID? Do you use my full name?"

Elena didn't say anything. Her first thoughts were weirdly defensive. Why wouldn't she have put in her full name? The phone asked for a first and last name when she created a contact. How would she know that her phone would one day find its way into the hands of an underground science experiment?.. Only slowly did she realize the gravity of what this meant. If they had Connie's name, they could easily narrow her down to the correct Constance Li. Of course, they would still need to find her address. And Connie was a fairly private person, so it wouldn't be easy to do. Unless…

"Connie, is your full CV posted online?"

Why wouldn't she have posted it online? Connie thought. All the blog posts said she needed to have a comprehensive online profile. What person in their right mind wouldn't have the most recent version up there? This was Elena's problem: she never went the extra mile in self-presentation. In fact—

"So—" Elena interrupted her train of thought. "—if it is posted, you redacted your home address, right?"

With a wordless exchange of glances, both friends got up and headed for the door.

The door to Connie's apartment opened onto an outdoor landing. She was on the second floor, and one could take one of two staircases (facing east or west) to reach the ground level. Either led out to an unfenced parking lot.

At first, Connie and Elena took the east staircase because this one led in the direction of Connie's car. But they had only made it a couple of steps when they saw a phalanx of owl-headed creatures in dark tunics blocking their way. When they doubled back and tried the west staircase they found a smaller line of Owls coming from the other direction. Either way they tried to run, there was a formation of silent Owls standing in their way. Their only option was to run back into the apartment, but before they could do so, they were apprehended by a pair of Owls they hadn't noticed hiding on the stairs leading up to the third floor. As they were held in place on the landing, Connie and Elena watched in horror as the east phalanx parted and a shadowy figure approached. As the figure stepped into the light coming from the landing they could see it was wearing a long robe and had a gigantic bull's head. When the creature reached them, it laid a hand upon each friend, and they immediately lost consciousness.

Part Three: Friday

CHAPTER TWENTY-ONE

When Sasha filled out her Spring semester schedule, one of her main priorities was to keep her Fridays and Mondays empty. As much as she enjoyed being at Bellwether, she wanted to have the option to spend long weekends away from campus. Depending on how other things went, this could be an opportunity to visit her occasional boyfriend at Penn State, or it could be a chance to visit her sister up in New York. In either event, Sasha was feeling the need to foster connections beyond the campus community and to explore her life outside her undergraduate incubator—and she would have been much freer to do so if her macroeconomics class didn't include mandatory weekly "lab" sessions, or if her professor had at least honored her request not to be placed in the Friday morning lab. But the scheduling gods had forsaken her. So instead of already being in Dumbo or State College, Sasha was now sitting in an overheated classroom listening to an adjunct professor explain how to adjust GDP to shifts in aggregate demand.

As she listened, Sasha became increasingly convinced of a conspiracy all around her. And it wasn't just the fact that the instructor kept telling the class to assume major aspects of the economy remained constant in order to simplify their equations (though that was also troubling), she was certain that something strange was happening closer to home, involving the Bellwether community. Though she had very little idea what was going on, Sasha was certain that it had something to do with both the Murray Otis lecture and the consulting firm the school had hired. She also suspected that Elena might know a little more about this than she had let on, and she was impatiently looking forward to meeting with her after class.

Sasha had started to feel suspicious while researching her article on the

Murray Otis lecture. As she had told Elena, the story behind inviting him seemed hazy to say the least, and she could only find vague and unreliable information about the Institute for a Better Society. They clearly didn't want much information to be available about them online. So next, Sasha decided to ask around at the College to see if there was anything unusual about the preparations being undertaken. The President's Office responded to her inquiries with a bland letter about the importance of promoting an open dialogue on campus. Most other campus offices gave similarly noncommittal statements, except the Dean of Students who agreed to meet with her. At first, this conversation was also fairly disappointing. The Dean stuck to platitudes about encouraging students to debate ideas while also providing necessary support for those who feel marginalized about Otis's views. Then, Sasha asked if she was afraid of violence at this event, and the Dean replied that it wouldn't be an issue since additional security forces would be on hand for the event. But when Sasha pushed for more details about whom exactly the school was hiring for security, the Dean backtracked, insisting that she only meant that the regular campus police would be advised of the potential risks related to this event. This reversal struck Sasha as odd, so she decided to investigate further. Campus police refused to comment officially, but one officer told Sasha off the record that he had heard they were bringing someone in from off campus, and it wasn't the local police, though he couldn't tell her any details beyond that. Running against a dead end with her campus sources, Sasha looked up articles on Otis's appearances at other campuses, and here she found something potentially interesting. In the student newspapers for multiple institutions she was able to find text to the effect that additional security was provided by a private firm. No name was offered, and the trail went cold.

There was a breakthrough in the case when an anonymous informant sent Sasha several messages on Hidechat. Identified only as Tito_Alba27, the user suggested that Sasha should look into the activities of some organization called Moahil Loch, alleging that they were the group who was in charge of additional security for Friday's event. This anonymous informant also warned Sasha that the group behind making these decisions was very dangerous. Though "Tito" wouldn't go into details, it sounded as though they had already taken steps of some kind to silence opposition on campus.

In her conversation with Elena yesterday, Sasha had confirmed that the administration had hired Moahil Loch as budgetary consultants. This in itself seemed odd to Sasha. As far as she could tell, Moahil was a private firm that advised various corporations on how to cut costs, and it wasn't clear that they had prior experience advising in higher ed. There was no direct mention of them providing security services on their website, though it was hard to verify anything from their website, which mainly featured a stunning array of business jargon and no real information about their services or clients. It also turned out that the only useful part of this website, the button for contacting a local representative, was a dead link.

Next Sasha tried calling the phone number provided on the website but she received only an automated message: "Thank you for contacting Moahil Loch. We are dedicated to reshaping the world for future generations. Join us in fostering a better society." There followed about a minute of quiet static, then: "If you would like to learn more about our corporate services, visit our website. You may contact a representative through our online portal." Of course, there was no functioning online portal so this was another dead end. But it was a curious one. After all, what kind of consulting firm would make themselves inaccessible to potential clients? Somehow this consulting firm and the similarly unreachable Institute for a Better Society were tied up with the Otis lecture, and they may have more far-reaching involvement in the College.

This was about as far as Sasha had got by the time she ran into Elena at the campus center. Their encounter only reinforced Sasha's sense that something was very wrong on campus. She had no idea who Elena's balding "colleague" was but she could tell that Elena was afraid of him. So when Sasha parted with Elena in the parking lot, she pretended not to notice this man standing in the shadow of Bellwether Hall. On the off chance that this was somehow connected to Moahil Loch or Otis, she decided to send a message to Tito_Alba27: "Weird jacked balding man harassing profs on campus. Know anything about that?" It was about two hours later when she received a response.

Tito_Alba27: Don't ask around about this. Man is dangerous.
Deathwalks@12am: Who is he?
Tito_Alba27: A kind of recruiter for Moahil Loch. He's been very active lately.
Deathwalks@12am: Recruiting for what?
Tito_Alba27: Not sure. But it's happening soon.
Deathwalks@12am: What's happening?
Tito_Alba27: Don't know. But they're talking about a "second site" during lecture tmrw. Will try to find out more.

That was all Sasha could get from "Tito."

So she had a lot to think about during her macro lab. Who were these people? What did they want from Elena? What was "happening soon"?

After macro, Sasha had walked halfway back to her dorm when she remembered that she had made an appointment to meet Elena at 11. She arrived at her office at 11:01, but the door was shut and no one responded when she knocked. It was strange for Elena to miss an appointment. Sasha waited around for another ten minutes and then asked after her at the Department office.

"Elena doesn't come in on Fridays, dear," Cristina responded.

"She asked me to meet her today at 11," Sasha said. "We made plans to meet just yesterday."

Just for a moment, Sasha thought she noticed a rare look of concern on Cristina's face, but her features quickly resumed their normal placid expression. "Well, I'm sure she wouldn't have forgotten about your meeting. Something else must have come up."

CHAPTER TWENTY-TWO

When Elena and Connie awoke, they were tied to chairs in the middle of a large room lit by florescent lights. There was a tarp spread beneath them (which Elena took to be a bad sign). Elena could see nearly a dozen other part-time faculty from the Humanities Division, all dressed in green tunics with owls embroidered on them, standing in front of her in a single line. She could also hear what sounded like Simon and Dana arguing behind her—an argument that ended when Dana loudly whispered, "They're awake now, you asshole." Next she heard some bustling back there and what sounded like a speaker switching on. Moments later a figure emerged from behind them wearing a lumpy black mask. It addressed them through a voice distorter:

"From time immemorial, cultures the world over have regarded the owl as a messenger between worlds. Under cover of night this avian seeker hunts for souls to be brought to the altar of sacrifice before the most powerful of the ancient spirits, the one dark lord in service of whom the order of Minerva was founded centuries ago and for whose sake we now return to the grounds of Bellwether. One of you will soon join the shadowy ranks of his priests. For—"

"Are you the guy from yesterday?" Elena interrupted him. "Simon, I think it was."

During the ensuing pause, Elena was pretty sure that she heard Dana's stifled laughter. Then, the distorted voice resumed:

"It is a matter of no importance who I am. Personal identity will soon cease to have meaning. When our lord returns to earth from the depths of Hell, he will bring its infinite fire with him unto this earth. Every worldly being will be transformed by the Eternal Flame of the one True Knowledge."

While Simon was talking, a nattily dressed man wearing tinted glasses walked into the room and placed his hand on Simon's shoulder. This man seemed extraordinarily confident, judging not only by his preening stride, but also by the fact that he seemed completely unselfconscious about the fact that he was trying to pull off a goatee with tiny handlebars under his pompadour haircut. Elena fervently wished her hands could be freed for a moment to smack him, and her desire to do so only increased as she heard him talk.

"Well, that was entertaining, wasn't it?" the man said, gesturing for Simon to return to his station. "Everything Simon said was more or less accurate, but I don't think words can adequately convey the gravity of this situation. For instance, if we were to tell you that both of you will die tonight, that would only make marginally more upset than you are currently. The words are just too abstract to have the necessary impact. But if I show you this," he held up a knife, "your pulse jumps quite a bit, and it will speed up even more if I do this—" He jammed the knife into Sandra's chest just below the right shoulder blade. Surprisingly, she hardly winced, and the cut hardly bled. "You see? Neither of you can help shuddering as you watch the knife cut into a person's skin. And it's similar with the coming of the one whom Simon calls our Lord. You really have to see it in person even to begin to understand its significance." Here, he made a dramatic pause. "Sadly, of course, neither of you will live long enough to see it with your mortal eyes—we can only hope your spirits catch a glimpse of His ascent before being cast into eternal torment."

"Who the hell are you?"

"Yes, where are my manners?" he smiled. "My name is Dr. Santiago Aguilar. Of course, I'm already well aware of both of you, so don't worry about introducing yourselves. Since we are on such familiar terms, I suppose I might as well admit that the 'Dr.' in my name is a little bit of an affectation. I actually dropped out of grad school before finishing my dissertation. Just didn't like the look of the job market. Pursued other opportunities."

"Why did you tell us that?" Connie asked.

"Now there's a creative question! I've never done this before—you're my first hostages to live this long—but I assume most people ask, 'What do you want from us?' Which is a really dumb thing to ask after someone announces they intend to kill you. Do you really think they are going to change their mind? Just seems arrogant to think that…"

"Do you always talk this much with your victims?" Elena asked.

"Hm." Santiago seemed to think about this one for a moment. "That one's a good question content-wise, but not so great pragmatically. What if I were to take it as a sign that you're feeling impatient with this conversation? Or that you doubt my resolve to kill you? Either interpretation really would be a problem for you."

"Fuck you," Connie offered.

(As an aside, it bears mentioning that Elena and Connie had actually discussed before what each of them would say if they were tied up together by a maniac. For the record, only the first of these questions went according to their plan.)

"Yes, that makes sense. At some point, these conversations must always devolve into hostility. Which is a shame! After all, you must have so many questions for me by now. I'll wager this is the first time either of you has been abducted by an organization of any kind, let alone a mysterious group with occult aspirations and what must look to you like the power to brainwash. There must be so many things you want to ask! Although…I suppose Constance is right that we best get on with things. You can't see him, Elena, but your old friend Ben is standing back there looking at his watch. And he's quite right! We have more preparations to make. But there's one question that I can answer for you without getting off schedule. I'm sure you're wondering what we've done to these fine folks here." He gestured at the row of part-time faculty behind them. "How do we get them to be so *pliant*? Well, I'll show you. Ben, please bring me the bowl."

Ben emerged next to Elena carrying an intricately decorated gold bowl. He held the bowl against her chest and tried to look away. Meanwhile, Santiago approached Elena brandishing the knife.

"Oh, Ben?" Santiago said. "Did you remember to treat the bowl with oil? Are you absolutely sure? Here let me see it." As Ben turned toward Santiago to show him the bowl, the latter swept his blade across Ben's neck in a swift and fluid motion. Grabbing the bowl in one hand and the back of Ben's neck in the other, he held his open veins over the bowl as he bled out. Once the bleeding had subsided, he laid Ben on his back with the bowl next to him. When he spoke next, he raised his voice and looked past Elena and Connie:

"Presence at the Summoning is a privilege. Remember this." Then he addressed Elena: "I don't apologize for the mess. It's appropriate that you should be marked with his blood, since you are the reason I had to do this. If Ben had done his job yesterday and brought you to our office, I wouldn't have had to drive out to Ms. Li's apartment in the middle of the night."

"You're fucking crazy," Connie shouted.

"You shouldn't throw labels around like that," Santiago responded. He knelt down beside Ben's body. "Especially since you'll be wondering about your own sanity in a couple minutes." He produced some kind of small box from his pocket, opened it, and started rubbing Ben's throat with some kind of salve. After a few minutes he called out, "No need to keep your eyes shut. You can look at it now. The cut's all fixed."

Indeed, there was now no sign of violence on Ben's neck—where there had been a grotesque slash, there was now fresh, healthy skin. Next,

Santiago said some words in an unfamiliar language and blew some kind of powder in Ben's face. His eyes and mouth suddenly opened—he didn't come back to life at this moment, the corpse just now had a gaping mouth and wide eyes. Santiago dripped a few drops of liquid into the bowl containing Ben's blood and then carefully started pouring it into the mouth of the corpse. When the bowl was empty, Santiago said a few more words in the unknown language and stepped away. "Now here comes the interesting part."

About a minute later, Ben started to move. At first, his body just kinda twitched involuntarily, then it shook violently for a bit, and finally the shaking subsided and Ben rose up off the ground. Slowly, unsteadily, he started walking around the room, as if he had no sense of direction. After a few minutes of wandering, he walked straight into Connie and fell over on top of her, flailing wildly, as if he was trying to run away but had forgotten how to do so. Santiago laughed at this before shouting in short, deliberate bursts: "Stop. Stand up. Join the file. Await reassignment." Upon hearing these commands, Ben froze (falling off Connie, onto the floor), got up, and walked over to join the line of tunic-wearing part-time faculty.

"So that's basically my end of it. You've already met Simon. He will finish things up once our friend Ben has had time to rest. Then, we'll grab him a tunic, and he'll be ready to join the ritual."

"What ritual?"

"A sacrifice to summon the Highest One to our earthly plane."

They tried to ask who this "Highest One" was, but Santiago would only aver that it was nothing they had to worry about. The world would know this being's incredible power soon enough, and really, the two of them should embrace the fact that nothing depended on them anymore—this might be the first and only time in their lives that they could truly live in the moment. Evidently pleased by his own cleverness, he made a great show of growing bored with their conversation and took his leave.

"Excuse me, sir," Simon called out. "What should we do with these two?"

"Well, there's no point killing them early," Santiago responded. "Let's just keep them here for the ritual. It's two less we'll have to gather. Speaking of which—" Santiago walked over and placed his hand upon Ben. "You stay here to await reassignment." He turned to his row of servants. "To the rest of you: Go forth and bring me five more offerings for tonight!"

CHAPTER TWENTY-THREE

So began the hunt.

***

The first to be picked up was a student worker. Solange was nearing the end of her morning shift when she overheard a student complaining about the soda fountain. She was on beverage duty, so she checked the fountain, and indeed, the cherry cola spout was spraying water with only a slight hint of brown coloring. That meant that the syrup must have run out.

So she headed downstairs to check on the problem. While walking down the basement hallway she was a little surprised that she could hear someone else down here—it was usually empty, especially on a Friday morning—but she thought nothing of it. It was probably just her manager checking on something. As she entered the soda stocking room, she picked up a box labeled "cherry cola" from the near wall. She looked at the wall of tubes leading up from this room to the soda machine, but she couldn't make out most of the faded labels. So she went to take a closer look at the syrup bags to see which one had run out. As she was crouched over examining the bags, she heard someone in the hallway again—evidently walking in her direction. Oddly, this time it sounded like two people. But again, she thought nothing of it and continued with her work. She had located the empty syrup bag and unscrewed the cap on the replacement when she heard the footsteps enter the room. Since she was so close to being finished, she quickly sealed the replacement bag in place before looking up and—

She wasn't exactly frightened when she looked up, just surprised. The two unfamiliar faces looking at her were too old to belong to students. It was a smallish, dark-haired man and a tall blond woman, neither of whom worked at the cafeteria. They were also wearing odd green outfits that she couldn't quite place. She really wasn't frightened at all, just intrigued by this strange pair, watching them with curiosity the whole time they were closing in.

***

The second student offering was gathered in the common room of the Botkin dormitory. During the daytime, the vast common area on the first floor of 'Chuckbot' was usually empty—that is, except for Rogelio Jimenez, who would go often go down there to get away from his roommate Subhash. While Rogelio liked Subhash for the most part, he hated his taste in music, especially on "Free Jazz Fridays" when Subhash liked to blast Sun Ra all afternoon. Rogelio would get away by going down to the first floor, which was just far enough away that he couldn't hear the cacophonic tonal liberation, and watching cartoons in the common room.

So as on most Fridays, Rogelio was lying on the couch half-asleep in front of the television. When he heard footsteps in the hallway, he assumed it was just some of his dorm mates coming home from lunch. He was surprised to hear the steps come into the common room at this time, but for a moment he didn't even look up. The newcomer was already standing over the couch when Rogelio finally raised his head.

He was surprised to see a middle-aged man standing over him. It wasn't one of his instructors, but for whatever reason still he felt a little embarrassed to be caught watching cartoons, and his first instinct was to make some kind of explanation for why he wasn't doing something more serious, like writing a lab report. Before he could say anything in his defense, however, he noticed the man's unusual raiment and decided that this probably was not a faculty member. He was about to ask what he was doing here when the man violently seized him with both hands and everything went black.

***

The third was caught by a lone Owl.

This Owl was stalking the southern part of the Bellwether campus. He didn't know exactly why he was there. Maybe he had been invited to give a lecture, or maybe he was meeting a friend. Whatever his reason for being there, he could only stay if he found a fitting candidate...a candidate for what?.. It wasn't a scholarship, but it was something very important. He didn't know why he was doing any of this, but he knew how to do it. He would find someone who fit the description, someone who was alone, someone he could overpower, and he would use the little cylinder in his pocket to make them be quiet. Then he would take them away.

The athletic facilities would be a good place to hunt. Only a few people would be there around midday. There would be a good candidate here.

(He didn't know how he knew this—to tell the truth, he didn't know how he knew most things at this point.)

He went to a doorway on the side of the main gym building where students would sometimes exit after finishing their workouts. (Again, how did he know this campus so well?) Sure enough, the door swung open after a few minutes. It was a young man leaving the locker room to go for a jog around campus; he was wearing headphones and didn't even look back to see that someone was holding the door open. Not wanting to cause a stir in the open air, the Owl stole into the athletic facility to continue the hunt.

The fitness center was mostly quiet this afternoon. The Owl walked around the row of elliptical machines, dispassionately surveying the young, athletic bodies in search of a suitable offering. But these machines were too crowded, and the students were watching him with obvious discomfort, so the Owl walked downstairs to the weight room instead. Perfect. In the far corner there was a lonely young man doing the military press with a bar and no spotter. The Owl quietly sidled over to him, stood behind the bench, and waited for the weight to lower to the young man's chest. Then, he gave the bar a quick downward push and pulled it back hard against the student's neck. As the student gasped for air the Owl stuck him with his syringe. He dragged the body out the back door just before a pair of lax bros came trotting down the stairs to work their lats and pecs.

***

On Fridays, Teddy Soplica worked in the College store. It was a slow day, most likely due to students preparing for the protests, and he found himself with about an hour left in his shift and nothing to do. He killed a bit of time on the floor—adjusting the stuffed barn owls, ordering some sweatshirts by size, and touching up the coffee mug display pyramid. Finally, he figured that it couldn't hurt to lay low for the rest of his shift, so he grabbed his Italian textbook and ducked into the storage room. He sat down on a footstool and started practicing conjugations.

There wasn't much chance of anything needing to be restocked today, meaning no one should be coming in to disturb him. But after about twenty minutes he was surprised to hear the door swing open. Assuming it was his manager coming to tell him that he was needed on the floor, he quickly hid his book and started to pretend to do inventory. He heard the door shut and was surprised to see that the newcomer hadn't moved from the doorway.

It wasn't his manager but a strangely dressed Indian woman with a nose ring and red highlights. "Excuse me. Can I help you?" he asked, but she didn't respond. He approached her slowly, explaining that customers shouldn't be in the storage area, but none of this provoked any reaction. Suddenly, when he got within a couple feet of her, she lunged at him, shoving him against a row of shelves. As he felt a barrage of pens and notebooks falling on him, he finally recovered from his shock and started pushing back. He was surprised how strong she was. Before he had gained much ground he felt—belatedly, moments after it actually happened—the pinprick at the base of his neck. Before he could figure out what had happened he felt that he was having trouble concentrating, that he wasn't really sure whether he still had the upper hand in this confrontation, or even where he was trying to go, and he started to stumble a little before he finally fell to the ground unconscious.

***

By one o'clock the Owls had caught four of the five offerings they were tasked to find.

***

Sasha liked to sit on the B level of the library. This floor was crowded with books; there were only a handful of work desks interspersed among the bookshelves. When she had first come to Bellwether, she found this floor claustrophobic, not to mention depressing, with its dim lights, abandoned book carts, and rows of bookshelves so closely packed that one had to move them with a hand crank to access the books. For a while she tried to avoid this area, working instead at the large and well-lit tables on the aboveground levels. But the group study spaces in the library were hardly ever used for group study. Instead, they acted primarily as dedicated areas for consorting with friends while making a show of studying. And after a while Sasha realized that the one major advantage to B level was that other students mostly avoided it for the same reason she did. So Sasha had acclimated herself to the claustrophobia and learned to enjoy its somber quiet.

Of course, she probably didn't have to be all the way down on B level today, since hardly anyone was in the library anyway… It was admittedly a little hard to concentrate, knowing that everyone else was taking the afternoon off. Sasha had intended to start working on her latest problem set for macro right away, but somehow she had taken out her laptop instead of her problem set and gone online instead of starting her work. After a little while she became so engrossed in various search windows and chat screens that she didn't notice someone else was walking around on B level. In fact, if she were listening, she could hear two sets of footsteps starting near the elevators and methodically walking down each aisle, until they reached about midway between Sasha and the elevators. Here, they stopped because they could hear someone typing, and after a moment they both took off in the direction of this noise.

Their quickened footsteps caught Sasha's attention. She looked up to see a middle-aged man and woman in green tunics coming towards her. By this point she was suspicious enough about everything happening at Bellwether that she didn't wait to see what these people wanted from her. Instead, she abandoned her laptop and dashed away from them along the northwest wall.

Her suspicions were immediately confirmed, as the woman followed her down the aisle at a quickened pace. The man was hung back. As Sasha walked along the southwest wall, she could catch glimpses of him through the open rows in the movable bookshelves. He was walking along the center pathway in pace with her, so that she wouldn't be able to escape down one of the aisles. Sasha quickly reviewed her options. There was no exit along this wall. She could try to hole up in the bathroom, but there was no window since she was below ground, and she wasn't optimistic that she could hold the door for very long. Instead, she made a break for the sorting area at far corner of the library, where there was a break in the stacks and she would have more room to maneuver.

The sorting area was a small square of space filled with pushcarts for returning books to the stacks. When Sasha reached this area, the woman was following close behind her, and the man who had been following from a distance now believed she was cornered and sprinted toward them. Sasha was able to buy a little distance by pushing one of the carts between herself and the woman. Then, she seized upon a second cart and pushed it in the woman's direction. This one knocked her back hard against the nearest bookshelf. Using a third cart for cover, Sasha doubled back in the direction from which she had come.

Now, Sasha had an advantage. Both of her pursuers were following from behind. She just needed to focus and she could make it out of here.

As Sasha ran back along the row of stacks, she quickly pulled out the locks that held several rows in place. Making a quick right-angle turn she ran up one of the open aisles with one of her pursuers following a couple yards behind her. When she reached the end of the row, she quickly wrenched the wheel that moved the shelves and crushed the man between two rows of shelves. As she expected, the woman tried to cut across the stacks a few rows down. Sasha spun this wheel too, sandwiching her second pursuant between the shelves. Although neither would be incapacitated for long, this was enough of a head start for Sasha to make it to the stairwell and run from the building.

With vague feelings of disappointment and confusion, the two Owls picked themselves up to return from the library and face the wrath of their Master. But just as they were about to reach the elevator, the door opened and another diligent student walked out to get some work done on B level. Before she could get distracted on the internet, the Owls were upon her.

CHAPTER TWENTY-FOUR

"I guess we should just 'reassign' him here, right?" Dana asked after about half an hour had elapsed. She indicated Ben, who had been standing motionless since Santiago left the room. The other zombie servants were gone now, leaving the awkward party of Simon, Dana, resurrected Ben, and the tied-up Connie and Elena in the room. They had been sitting in silence since Santiago left.

"Yeah, I'll get the equipment," Simon said. "You okay watching these two on your own?"

"Um, yeah. I'm sure I'll be fine," Dana scoffed. "The ropes do most of the work."

She was right about that. Both Connie and Elena were stuck sitting very uncomfortably with their hands tied behind their backs and their legs tied together. It was a situation that each of them had watched countless heroes escape in movies, but they couldn't figure out how to do it in real life. As much as Elena tried to visualize herself dislocating her joints slipping her hand free, as much as she strained her fingertips toward loose ends she imagined in the rope, nothing came out of her efforts.

But maybe there was a psychological technique that could get them out? Maybe one of their captors was a weak link, who could be convinced to let them out?... Looking at Dana, Elena remembered her first impression of her. She seemed so much younger than Simon or Santiago, so much cooler; a little caustic, perhaps, but no so much so that she didn't have a sense of humor or the ability to relate to a similarly cool hostage... Dana probably didn't want to be caught up in this whole thing. They must be forcing her to go along with it. But she could totally turn the tables on them if given the right push. Maybe now that Simon was out of the room...

"Dana?" Elena called out. "Listen, Dana. I think—or actually, I believe I *know* that you don't want to be involved in this. You're probably afraid of

Simon and that Santiago guy. And I don't *blame* you at all for going along with it. I'm sure it's been very difficult. But maybe, while they are out of the room, you could just, you know, let us go?"

"Oh, well… Sure - I would totally let you two go if it were up to me."

"But it *is* up to you!" Elena suddenly felt hopeful. "No one else is in the room right now. They don't have to find out…"

"Oh! No, that's not what I meant." Dana sounded genuinely surprised that Elena could have misinterpreted her words. "By 'if it were up to me' I just meant 'if things were different,' or maybe in this case it could be translated as 'if I wanted to.' It's just an expression—something you say to be polite." Dana checked something on her phone, then asked: "Do you really think I'm afraid of Simon? He bought a Halloween mask and a voice distorter just to talk to you! Sure, Santiago's a different story, but he won't be back for hours."

"Then, why are you doing this to us?"

"Okay, I might as well tell you. You see…I made a sweet deal with the Dark Lord. (Or the 'Highest One' or whatever you want to call him.) When He comes to claim his kingdom, I will be a ruler of my own fiefdom. But most importantly, He will be give me a new, indestructible metal body with gnarly weapons all over it."

"You want to be part metal?"

"So bad! I've been wanting to be something more than merely human ever since reading the 'Cyborg Manifesto' in Freshman Seminar" a couple years ago.

("You see, Connie? I told you first-years don't get Haraway!" *This is anecdotal evidence at best.* "How am I supposed to conduct a survey while tired to a chair?" *"Anyway, it sounds like she didn't read the text at all and just made up her own narrative based on the title."* "That's the whole problem! Students need context to understand that kind of complex rhetoric. Even if they read it at that stage, they end up just filling in their own content behind the unfamiliar words.")

"Guys! Come on. I totally got what Haraway was saying. I just put my own spin on it. You need to ask what came *before* the human: all-powerful gods and demons. That's where the real power's at. Who cares about theory, when I can have real power over my own realm in the fiery kingdom of our eternal master!"

"Okay, this is just bull—"

"Connie!" Elena hissed. "Let me try to talk to her. Okay, Dana, it sounds like you've put a lot of thought into this, and we're not trying to judge your life choices. But have you thought about the other people this affects?"

"We've killed thirteen people just this week. I think I get it."

"But maybe you only saw all of them as faceless victims. And now that you've had a chance to talk to us, you see us—or at least one of us—as something more than that? Maybe even…I don't know—as a friend?"

"You're being very egotistical right now," Dana responded. "We care about all of our victims equally."

"That's reassuring," Connie said. "If you're not going to free us, could you at least answer something for me? Why do you need the part-time faculty to help with this plan?"

"Oh, no reason. We just needed bodies. In principle, it could have been anyone." Dana gestured toward Ben, who kept lightly swaying on his feet. "Santiago told us to target the adjuncts. Between you, me, and the zombie, I think he has his own baggage there."

"But why send them to Wanesdale?" Connie asked. "If you were just creating zombie servants, what was the point of sending them to another college for the day?"

"Oh," Dana responded, as if surprised it wasn't obvious. "There's actually a really good reason for that. You see—"

At this point, she was interrupted by Simon, who needed help carrying a large black suitcase into the room. He squatted near Ben, opened the case, and took out a syringe and a small black tablet. He stuck Ben with the syringe in the thigh and unloaded its contents. Then, he started tracing figures on the tablet with a stylus. After a couple minutes, Elena and Connie heard a *ding* and saw Simon reach back into his suitcase. He pulled out what looked like an electric wand and waved it around Ben's head a few times. Suddenly, Ben became much more animated, looking around with a confused expression, stamping his feet in place for a moment, and then—he lunged forward and started to slap Simon hard in the face.

"See?" Simon yelled to Dana after the first few blows. "And that's why we always use restraints! These stupid things are so quick to pan—" Now Ben was holding Simon by the throat with both hands. The latter hit Ben with the wand and momentarily broke away. Scrambling, Simon picked up the tablet again and made a few more signs over it. Ben grabbed him by the shoulder. Simon made a more frantic gesture and Ben suddenly hung his head and arms in a manner that reminded Elena of a robot being shut off on TV.

After he had caught his breath, Simon made a squiggle gesture over the tablet and then tapped. A moment later, he tried the same gesture again. And again. Ben was unresponsive.

"What did you do?" Dana asked, actually sounding a little alarmed. "Don't tell me you did what I think you did."

Simon didn't respond. He kept playing with the tablet for a minute and then started rummaging in his suitcase. He strapped something around the top of Ben's head and ran over him with the wand a few times. Nothing happened. Simon was becoming more and more visibly irritated. After a few more attempts to fiddle with the tablet and the wand, he punched Ben on the shoulder in frustration, knocking him straight to the floor. Next, he pulled a small knife out of his pocket and jammed it into Ben's thigh. There was still no movement, not even a twitch.

After staring at Ben for about thirty seconds, Simon straightened up and addressed Dana: "Okay, we're going to fix this. We just need to grab a little powder from the other room."

"Okay, you go," Dana responded. "I'm not about to mess with Santiago's stuff. You saw what he did to Ben just for falling a little behind."

"Yes, well, there are plenty of things I could tell him about your work lately. Or maybe you would like to explain Subject 11's lazy eye? Or even better, how this one here ran right by you last night in the operating room?"

Dana begrudgingly agreed to go with him. Evidently, she did not want to risk displeasing Santiago before acquiring her new metal body from their unnamed demon lord.

When Simon and Dana had left the room, Connie and Elena immediately realized that this was their chance to escape. They just couldn't quite figure out how to do it. First they tried a trick they had seen in movies, where they turned their chairs around so that they were sitting back to back. Since each had her hands tied behind the back of the chair, this would hypothetically have allowed them to untie each other—if it weren't so damn hard to untie a knot with your hands bound. Next, Connie had the idea of ramming their chairs into each other in the hopes of breaking the chair frames. Unfortunately, this only succeeded in knocking them both onto the ground. Finally, they resolved on making a break for the door while still tied to the chairs. Moving in this fashion was extremely frustrating and even painful, as the ropes cut off circulation whenever they moved. Still, at least they were making progress. Very slow progress. When they had come about even with Ben, Elena heard Connie call out:

"Look!"

Ben was moving again now. He couldn't quite stand himself up, but he had got onto his knees and was twitching there.

He must have been in some kind of shock before, Connie reasoned. Now that he was awake, maybe they could use him to escape. "Ben. Untie the cord around my hands."

Ben dutifully stumbled his way over and started clumsily pawing at the knot. It was useless. She might as well have been asking a cat in boxing gloves to undo the knot. Then she remembered something.

"Ben! Pull the knife out of your thigh. Use the knife to cut the rope." After a second's thought she added: "Make sure not to cut my arm."

Once again, Ben dutifully complied, clumsily but effectively cutting the rope. Connie ordered him to give her the knife and undid her own legs before running over to free Elena.

Together, they ran out the door into a poorly lit hallway. It was a gray, mostly anonymous space, but certain details—the shape of the door handles, the locations of the bathrooms—looked vaguely familiar to Elena. She felt like she had been in this space in different lighting, though she couldn't place it. Only when they made it to the stairs did Elena recognize they were in the basement of Howlsley Hall.

"We're at Bellwether," she called out.

"I hate your school," Connie responded.

They ran upstairs into the building's atrium. Under different circumstances, Elena had always liked this area. It felt very stately with its wooden floors and paneling, not to mention the musty old bookshelves rumored to have been transferred from David Howlsley's home library. At the moment, however, she was unable to enjoy the decor as they were running through it at a mad dash. If she had been paying more attention, Elena would have seen that the building was in rare form this afternoon, with geometric symbols drawn in white chalk on the floor, a crate containing owl masks sitting in the atrium, and seven large wooden stakes piled up in the hallway.

But Elena and Connie didn't see these things. Instead, they ran for the front door, not knowing this door had been locked and was additionally watched by two hired security guards ordered to prevent anyone from escaping. When the door wouldn't open for them, they sprinted across the atrium, hoping now to escape by the back door. Before they got to this door, however, it opened of its own accord and six Owls walked in.

"Found them!" Dana shouted out somewhere behind them. Moments later they were each seized by two owls and brought to the center of the atrium. At this point, Connie also recognized the building from past visits.

"Jesus Christ, Elena. What are we doing in your department?"

CHAPTER TWENTY-FIVE

David Leland Howsley III was a thorough scholar, a dedicated teacher, a capable administrator, and a fastidious dresser. So attested his friends, his colleagues, and even a blurb on the website for Bellwether College. By every account, he was an exceedingly careful individual, observing the utmost degree of proprietary in every interaction and showing the highest diligence in his professional functions. And so, it is all the more surprising that his legacy has been plagued by rumors of involvement in occult rituals and perhaps even murder.

According to these rumors, Howlsley's suspicious activities began as a result of his research. He had long been fascinated by the history of sacrificial rites, especially the psychological experience of participants in religions that demand extraordinary sacrifices from their devotees. Through his research into this topic Howlsley became increasingly interested in a small Canaanite religion that practiced especially brutal forms of discipline and human sacrifice. The practitioners of this religion were known for their rigid internal hierarchy, which informed their social structure and sacrificial practice. The senior circle of priests would make all decisions about the day-to-day life of the worshippers in accordance with their interpretation of a series of arcane rules passed on from generation to generation. Once a year they would perform a massive sacrifice of their younger acolytes, who would be offered up to a giant furnace in the shape of their terrible god. Although this ritual has often been mischaracterized as an act of child-sacrifice, the offerings were actually all young adults who had made unsuccessful bids to join the priesthood. Try as he might, Howlsley could not find any information about why certain acolytes succeeded in joining the priesthood while others failed—it was at the least an exceedingly opaque process, if not a wholly arbitrary one. For those who survived, induction into the upper ranks was celebrated with the elaborate ritual of

Ten-Yur, in which they were paraded around in robes and anointed with the blood of a slaughtered calf to symbolize their rebirth among the ruling class. From this point forward, they would be invulnerable to sacrifice and regarded as nearly unimpeachable authorities on cultic affairs.

Howlsley increasingly devoted his studies to this group, believing that their devotional practice must reveal much about the human instinct for subservience and the psychological need to perceive intrinsic value underlying a largely arbitrary hierarchy. At first, he did not take this group especially seriously, considering their practices only an intriguing case study in what he was beginning to call in his head a kind of psychological history of religious sacrifice. But as he unearthed more documents related to the group, and as he spent long hours with them trying to penetrate the mind of an acolyte, something strange began to happen to him. He found himself abstaining from any of the many recorded names to reference the god of this cult, as if he himself had committed to observing the strict taboo observed among its members. Instead, he would refer to this being as simply the "Highest One," in imitation of a medieval heretic who had discovered this cult many centuries later and managed to hide coded references in the religious texts he copied. Even though he did not initially believe in this being, there was something fascinating about the Power it represented and the obedience it commanded. As much as he professed to loathe blind subservience, he couldn't deny its psychological appeal; indeed, he himself felt attracted by the notion that one could partake in absolute Power through the simple act of total devotion. For reasons he didn't fully understand, Howlsley also began to wonder whether this Canaanite god was merely a symbol, and not, well, a real force active in the universe.

Over the course of these studies, he came upon the writings of a sixteenth-century Spanish mystic who claimed to have participated in resurrecting this cult in secret. Most intriguingly, this mystic claimed that the sixteenth-century reincarnation was actually superior to the original cult, as the ancient acolytes had misunderstood the prophecies, and therefore sacrificed countless lives in vain. In fact, the coming of the "Highest One" was not meant to happen in their lifetime but many generations later through the actions of a figure known only as "the Scholar," who would rediscover the cult's teachings and bring them to fruition. (The mystic believed himself to be this figure.) The "Highest One" would be manifest on this earth through a sacrifice of seven innocent souls in an elaborate ceremony conducted by twelve priests and a single bishop. Once these souls had been committed to flame, the bishop and his most loyal followers would usher in a new era of humanity, ruled by the unerring hand of this eternal spirit.

At this point, Howlsley began to feel certain that dedication to this being was more than merely a curious psychological phenomenon. He understood this prophesy as a dire promise, which he himself would help to fulfill. Of course, he was humble enough to realize that he was not the prophesied Scholar. His role was more likely that of a "Messenger" or "Intermediary," one of the chosen few who were prophesied to pass the teachings of the cult into the hand of the one who would deliver humanity into the hands of the "Highest One."

Howlsley's realization of his own profound historical importance roughly coincided with the appearance of Anna Sowa in his life—and the only real scandal to tarnish his reputation. At this time, it was observed that Howlsley was making frequent trips to Philadelphia with an unknown motive and without the accompaniment of his wife. Rumors began to circulate after Howlsley was observed in the bohemian parlor of a certain Anna Sowa, whose reputation for hosting immoral gatherings was well known among the Bellwether faculty. Concurrently, people started seeing a lot less of Mrs. Howlsley, and one close family friend had witnessed a frightful argument between the two shortly after one of Mr. Howlsley's trips to Philadelphia. Shortly after this argument, Mrs. Howlsley stopped appearing with husband entirely and any inquiry after her received the curt reply that she no longer lived at their shared residence.

The most common inference made from these events was a simple tale of marital infidelity. Upon learning that her husband was having an affair with Sowa, Mrs. Howlsley had confronted him, and when he refused to break off the relationship, she had left him to live with relations elsewhere. The couple would have kept the matter to themselves in the interest of propriety, especially considering Howlsley's position as President of the College. Although this mundane explanation was entirely plausible, it was an era when all types of lurid fiction enjoyed great popularity, and an especially malicious rumor circulated to the effect that Howlsley had done away with his wife in a quiet fashion, perhaps by slipping arsenic or some similar poison into her food. Yet this was by no means the most extreme suggestion that was made. Some people claimed that Sowa was, in fact, no mere eccentric but someone who was in actual contact with dark spiritual forces. There were allegations that Howlsley too believed in Sowa's powers and had made her his personal spiritual adviser, perhaps in the hopes that she could establish contact for him with the divinity of the cult he had spent so long studying. Wherever the truth in these matters lay, the notion that Howlsley had taken up with Sowa in one way or another was all but confirmed by the events following Mrs. Howlsley's departure. At this time, Howlsley resigned from his post at the College, and Anna Sowa broke ties with her friends and associates in Philadelphia, disappearing as if into thin air.

For the most part, the rumors about Howlsley were quick to die out in the years following his death. He was remembered as an upstanding member of the College community and a faithful steward during his time in the administration. Nonetheless, the stories of his occult practices cropped up in an odd way about two decades after his death. This was when Pete Rossetano, at the time a recent graduate of Bellwether College, claims he first heard "the Voice" warning him of impending danger. Pete would never give details about what the Voice sounded like or exactly what it said, and he was always cagey regarding the situations in which it spoke. All he would say of the first occurrence was that he was cocky in his early days; he was engaged in some things he shouldn't have been doing, and his activities had crossed some guys you didn't want to cross. The Voice had intervened at an important moment, when he was supposed to be at a certain place at a certain time to make a very valuable deal, and it had told him to get the heck out of Dodge instead. Pete listened and never looked back, but he had a business associate who did attend this meeting, and things didn't go too well for him. This convinced him to keep listening to the Voice going forward. Town after town, deal after deal—he always knew exactly when to jump out of the pot. (This earned him his nickname, "Slippery" Pete Rossetano.) Over the years, he came to have total confidence in the Voice and follow its directives without question. So when it told him to found the Lodge of the Owl at Sowa's house in Philadelphia, he didn't hesitate. By this time, Pete was a wealthy man, and the Lodge was an exclusive club, frequented by Philadelphian high society, as well as some finance lawyers from Wilmington. The core circle of members was made up a group of Bellwether alumni who had also allegedly been called by the Voice.

This Lodge had one simple mission: to resurrect the "Highest One" by any means necessary. This meant employing the wealth and extensive connections of its members to ready things for the coming of the "Scholar." Thus, the Lodge of the Owl began the process of infiltrating Bellwether long ago. It was they who donated money to the library to see to the preservation of Howlsley's papers, which also resulted in the one portrait commissioned during his lifetime being hung over the entryway. They also oversaw the construction of David L. Howlsley Hall, decorating the atrium with wood paneling and furniture donated by the Howlsley's estate, while also secretly reburying the body of the building's namesake beneath the foundation. Of course, alumni in the Lodge were also instrumental to the campaign to have Minerva the Owl replace Bellwether as the school's mascot. The ongoing financial crisis affecting the college for nearly a decade now had greatly expanded the Lodge's power over the College. It was a cohort of Lodge members who had founded the Moahil Loch consulting firm as a way of gaining access to the Bellwether administration. They had come up with an exceedingly simple operation, involving only a web designer and a couple representatives capable of giving convincing slide presentations to the administration. The brilliant insight that allowed them to get away with plan was simple: As long as they presented the administration with the results they wanted to see, suggesting heavy cuts where they already wanted to make them, no one would question their numbers. One of the orchestrators had made similar financial presentations for a pharmaceutical company, and so many of the slides that Moahil Loch showed to the administration were just slides from these old presentations with the names of offices at Bellwether substituted in. Once they were certain that no one would question their "data," the Lodge members started inserting joke slides just to see how much they would get away with (including, of course, the squatting creature with devil horns that Elena had noticed earlier).

About a year ago, the Lodge had learned that the Scholar was found. Since that time, they had dedicated their considerable resources to helping him cover up his comings and goings as he prepared for the ritual. Now, on Friday March 10, everything was finally in place. The Scholar reported that there had been a couple snags in the final preparations, but none of them posed any risk of deterring their plans.

CHAPTER TWENTY-SIX

Elena generally skipped the infrequent university-wide professional development events sporadically organized by various go-getters at the College to pad their resumes. If she had attended the "Understanding the Student of Today" roundtable last October, however, she would have learned that students today don't check email as often as she assumed. Evidently, students today primarily communicated with various newer types of messaging that Elena didn't really understand; in fact, a majority of the students who participated in the roundtable professed to prefer receiving even official communications about class via text or social media, rather than by email. This wouldn't have changed her teaching practice—catering to students' preferences to this extent seemed like unnecessary coddling, and she didn't have time to learn how to use a new app every couple years—but it might have made her think twice about her contingency plan of the previous night. To make sure they would be found if something happened, Elena had borrowed Connie's laptop before fleeing the apartment and composed a quick email to the one person she had been planning to see the next day.

As it happened, however, Sasha didn't check her email until her trip to the library after lunch, mere moments before she was attacked. By that time, Elena's email was buried under various other message, including a special offer from Amazon, an email from the President's office imploring everyone to observe a free and open dialogue, a heap of notifications from the macro course website, and an advertisement for an essay-writing service. She almost closed the tab before seeing an email from Elena with subject line URGENT!!!!! The email was short:

Dear Sasha,

If I don't come to office hours at 11am tomorrow, call 911. Tell them to send officers to 237 Prospect Pike. Give them the names "Moahil Loch" and "International Horizons."

Best, [sic!]
EM

Upon seeing the name "Moahil Loch," Sasha immediately sent a message to Tito_Alba27 asking about International Horizons. She simultaneously dialed 911 on her phone, forgetting that there was no cell service on B level. She could already hear the suspicious footsteps coming in her direction, so without time to think she quickly typed a second message to Tito_Alba27 saying simply "liBRARY HELP." She didn't have any real idea how "Tito" would help her in this situation—or more generally who this "Tito" was or what was happening in the library. But this message was all she could manage in the second before she took off along the stacks.

A few minutes later, when Sasha had successfully made it out of the library, she felt so overcome by her ordeal that she practically collapsed on the library steps. It was the warmest day so far this week, and students were casually milling around campus. Sasha felt so strange being in this familiar place, surrounded by familiar sights, but suddenly feeling it all to be alien and threatening. It was as if the campus was putting on a show, only pretending to be the same cheerful and welcoming place.

Sasha dialed 911 on her phone. "Campus security," the voice on the other end of the line answered. "How may I direct your call?" She hung up and tried again, only to have her call redirected a second time. Her next thought was simply calling out for help to whoever was around. But she wasn't sure whom she could trust on this campus anymore. There were several navy "security" jackets walking hurriedly across the quad. Sasha figured these must be the extra private police that the school hired for the Murray Otis lecture, and all the more reason not to yell out. So Sasha just sat on the steps for a couple minutes in a kind of paralysis, unable to think of anything to do next.

It was then that Sasha saw, hiding in the shadow of the library building, a slightly hunched man wearing tight black jeans and a leather jacket. He was awkwardly pacing with his hands in his pockets, and every few moments he would look over in her direction. On a hunch, she walked over to him.

"Tito?" she asked.

"Midnight Death Walker?"

As it turned out, his real name was Athanasius Wurdalac Donovan IV. (He went by Nate.) He worked for campus security and had recently noticed a lot of strange behavior in his office since Moahil Loch became involved with the College. His worst suspicions were confirmed earlier this week when he substituted for a colleague in transporting a "suddenly ill" faculty member to a "medical facility" on Prospect Pike. He was sent over to the South Lot, where he helped a thickset, balding man carry a blond woman down to the campus security building on a gurney. They loaded her onto a van parked outside. When they arrived at a little office building off the road, they drove around the back of the building and carried the gurney up a ramp to the backdoor, where they were met by an avuncular man with silly-looking hair and burning black eyes. By making small talk with the balding man on the way to and from the campus, Nate was able to determine that this wasn't the first person who had been delivered to this facility in this fashion. Yet the man was strangely reticent about everything else, and Nate couldn't help feeling a little suspicious about his driving partner's role in this instructor's sudden illness.

At the very least, Nate felt certain that others were in danger and he would have to watch his own step. Careful not to disclose his own identity, he had taken every opportunity that presented itself to pass the little he knew onto others investigating this situation. Nate wouldn't go into details about the measures he had taken so far, even though Sasha pressed, but he assured her that there was no more a reasonable person in his position could do.

Sasha felt a little disappointed in Nate. He didn't live up to the image of a clever, cloak-and-dagger "Tito" that had formed in her mind. It's likely that she would have had a more charitable opinion later in life, after her standards for other persons had been blunted by more years of adulthood, after life's inevitable disappointments had forced her to come upon the limits of her own abilities and question her own idealism. Then, she would have been glad to have any secret ally the universe would give her. But for now, she was still young enough to have impossibly high standards, and she had expected more of this anonymous informant who had seemed to know so much about what was happening on the Bellwether campus. She wouldn't have called out to this person for help if she knew he was just a clueless security guard, a timid bungler who saw his entire role as clumsily helping other, bolder people investigate his suspicions.

Disappointment aside, however, at least she had someone to talk to now. Nate wasn't the greatest, but he was also the only person she could definitely trust at the moment. Maybe he could be useful.

"Do you have any ideas on what all this is for?" Sasha asked him. "Someone has gone out of their way to invite a speaker no one likes. They have added a crazy amount of security to campus. There's some kind of group that seems to be abducting faculty members. I was just attacked in the library, and they are redirecting all 911 calls to campus security. Any idea on how it comes together?"

"No idea," Nate admitted. "There must be some way it all ties back to the lecture."

"Or maybe there isn't." If she was being honest, Sasha just said this to be contrarian. She still felt a little annoyed that Nate wasn't the clever operative she imagined, and she just felt like arguing against anything he said. But then, she thought about it for a minute and realized she may have hit on something. "Maybe there isn't," she repeated. "Maybe it doesn't all tie together. What if the lecture is just a diversion? What if they were just trying to divert our attention from what's really going on?"

"And what's that?" Nate asked.

Sasha had to admit this was a fair question. She still didn't have a plausible suggestion for what was going on. At this point, she only felt sure that it wasn't happening at Gorobec Hall where the lecture was scheduled. But where?.. Then, she remembered the security guards she had seen walking past the library. They were walking toward the highway, which was also away from Gorobec Hall. Where were they going?

"Do you know where they've assigned extra security today?"

Nate didn't know for certain. But he also suggested that he could find out by volunteering for an extra shift at 4pm. Even though they had brought in several people from Moahil Loch, they were still requesting additional Bellwether personnel take on overtime for the Otis lecture. Nate could message Sasha and let her know where else they had people stationed.

"Okay. And when will Otis be here?"

"He should be getting here around 3:30. He has a meeting with a philosophy professor before his lecture. We are supposed to send some people to escort him between the buildings at 4:30."

Back in her dorm room, Sasha quickly changed into a black blazer and a gray skirt. She worked her hair into an uncomfortable bun and practiced projecting "confident young conservative" into the mirror for a few minutes, reciting phrases like "trickle down" and "market solution" over and over again. Around four o'clock, Nate sent the message "Howlsley Hall," and Sasha charged confidently over to the philosophy building, where she waited outside until an angry little man, whose face matched the pictures she'd found online, walked outside to puff a cigarette.

"Mr. Otis? Sasha Banks, vice chairperson of the Young Aristotelians. It is such a pleasure to meet you finally." He didn't respond right away, so she took a deep breath and added: "I'm a great admirer of your work on the importance of traditional family structures to Black America." This seemed to put him at ease, as he looked up and offered his hand. "They asked me to pick you up early for your lecture. It's due to security concerns. If you don't mind, you can follow me over to the venue now. You can meet with some of the other Young Aristotelians there."

Otis mumbled something in response. He gestured airily with his cigarette that he was ready to go.

Sasha wasn't sure how much Otis knew about the layout of the campus. She figured it would be best to distract him just in case he knew they were walking away from Gorobec. "I wanted to mention how much I admire your recent article in *Firebrand*. Other people are so afraid to speak the truth about same-sex adoption, but you don't let compassion get in your way. You correctly expose the, er, well, you know the reasons better than I!"

Otis mumbled for a little while.

"Yes, that's an excellent way to put it! Clearly, if a chair has four legs, a same-sex couple can't raise a child. Such a beautiful distillation of the…purposes behind the logic of…" Sasha her voice kept getting softer. Otis looked preoccupied with his cigarette, and she really hoped he wasn't actually listening as her sentence ended within an involuntary rise on the words "social cohesion?"

Otis looked somewhat more annoyed than before. Once again he mumbled something.

"Oh—they didn't tell you? There was a change of venue. We're going to Howlsley Hall instead. There's also a very large auditorium there."

More mumbling.

"Yes, absolutely. It's wrong for them to move you. The administration is clearly submitting to pressure from liberals, and it makes me sick."

Sasha sent a text to several of the protest organizers she had interviewed for her article. The message read: "Just confirmed Otis lecture moved to Howlsley Hall. Have eyes on him and Young Aristotelians heading into new venue now. Redirect here now."

If someone was trying to keep the Bellwether students away from Howlsley Hall, they would have to deal with them now. Of course, Sasha still had no idea what she would be facing when she actually arrived at the building.

CHAPTER TWENTY-SEVEN

Santiago had first learned of Howlsley while still a grad student. At the time, he was researching the religious heritage of American institutions of higher education as part of a broader inquiry into the double meaning of the phrase "academic discipline." The central question of his dissertation was how the self-disciplining of religious practice related to the organization of the university. His adviser had suggested that he look into the legacy of David Howlsley at Bellwether, not so much because he was an especially influential figure, but because there was a large and unexplored trove of documents waiting to be studied in the special collections of Ercoli library.

So Santiago had applied for funding and arranged a summer research trip to Bellwether. When he first arrived at the library access office, he was informed that most of the regular library staff were away for the summer, but if he arrived at noon the following day, someone would be happy to walk him through the procedure for accessing the archive. Returning the following day, Santiago was surprised that he wasn't asked to fill out forms or show ID, but was instead taken to a small room in the basement filled with various knickknacks. Here, he was informed that one item in the room had belonged to David Howlsley, and Santiago would be able to access the papers if, and only if, he could identify the item on his first try. Assuming this to be a joke, Santiago simply indicated the first object that caught his attention, a side table with a marble top and cloven hooves for feet, and was astounded to be told that this table had, in fact, sat at Howlsley's bedside for the last two decades of his life.

Even more surprisingly, the furtive and efficient man who had just administered this test now led him up to the special collections reading room and informed him that he would have full access to Howlsley's papers. When Santiago asked to see a catalogue, the man informed him that he wouldn't be needing one and should just wait right here. A few minutes later, the man returned with a box of documents and dropped them on Santiago's desk, proclaiming that this would undoubtedly be the best place to start.

At this point, Santiago was beyond arguing, so he simply started to go through the files. There were astrological charts, intricate designs for some kind of tunic, detailed descriptions of rituals, transcriptions of chants… It took nearly an hour before he realized what he was looking at, but when he finally understood its purpose he couldn't help but smile. This was essentially a carefully put together guide to summoning an ancient Canaanite god, whose reign of fire and pain would bring eternal life and dominion over the mortal realm to those who had the faith to summon him through an act of human sacrifice.

In a way, Santiago found this plan endearing. After years of difficult study trying to understand the complex mechanisms underlying systems of power, he actually liked the simplicity of Howlsley's aspirations. Here was someone who just wanted to resurrect an ancient demon in order to become an immortal king. Who didn't at least somewhat sympathize with that goal? Maybe the rest of us set our sights lower, but we all have at least some thirst for distinction and a propensity to dedicate ourselves to those who can bestow it. For instance, if he were really honest with himself, Santiago would have to admit that one of the main reasons he got into academia in the first place was the status it accorded. There was something very attractive in the idea of being *the* expert in something, a person whose authority could not be challenged, at least within their own circumscribed area of expertise. But why limit oneself to being a petty tyrant over some infinitesimal outgrowth on a single branch of human knowledge? If Howlsley was right, Santiago mused, it was possible to research one's way to real power, to controlling the actions of a great part of humanity under the appointment of a demon lord.

At first, Santiago thought of Howlsley's attempts to contact this ancient god as a charming absurdity, and perhaps also a fruitful avenue of research. If he couldn't think of a way to work it into his dissertation, he could probably frame this as a standalone article. (Maybe it could be a case study of the return to occult mysticism as a reactionary anti-positivism among fin-de-siecle intellectuals—he would just need to find a somewhat counterintuitive way of theorizing Howlsley's obsessions, and this could be a successful article!) Over time, however, the nature of his interest in Howlsley began to change. It happened slowly. By imperceptible degrees he became more and more interested in the content of the papers he was studying. Rather than simply looking for material that would fit into his project, he became increasingly interested in how Howlsley conceptualized this demon and how exactly he meant to go about contacting it. He traced Howlsley's geometrical sketches with his finger and silently mouthed his incantations, trying to recreate the exact steps by which Howlsley had hoped to contact this demon.

For reasons Santiago never fully understood, he also felt increasingly self-conscious about his research. He kept checking over his shoulder to see if someone was watching him. This concern may have begun as a product of simple embarrassment: he didn't want anyone to see that he was so deeply invested in these strange symbols. But it slowly crept up to a point of constant paranoia. He would turn around in his chair several times an hour, convinced that someone was reading the manuscripts over his shoulder. After a while, he stopped turning around, although he continued to distinctly sense someone standing just behind his chair. Sometimes he would even hear a low whispering, though he could never make out more than a word or two at a time. He determined there were two voices: one speaking in oddly inflected English and the other speaking in a low hiss that he couldn't parse into individual words. He began to feel the sensation of someone standing behind him even after he left the archive, and he kept hearing the hissing more and more frequently. While it didn't speak words exactly, he could tell that it was trying to communicate something important. He just needed to train his mind to interpret it.

Around this time Santiago became increasingly concerned with the portrait of Howlsley in the lobby. Why was the owl so large? He didn't believe that it was simply an idiosyncratic choice by the artist. Howlsley wanted to communicate his message to a future scholar, and there had to be some way in which this portrait contributed. Should the owl be read as a symbol? Could it be something so simple as knowledge? Or was it a more specific allusion to mythology or folklore? Strangely, whenever Santiago stared at the owl in the portrait, the hissing become louder, more distinct. He could almost make out words in it. After a few minutes standing by the portrait, he would return to his work in the archive with renewed vigor. What had seemed like arduous work was suddenly easy, as if someone else were drawing the connections for him and instructing him on how to read the texts. Slowly, he lost all sense of his original research questions and pursued only one thing: the state of David Howlsley as he was writing these documents. He strove to reread everything Howlsley had read and to recreate every step of his reasoning. To this end, he devoted himself to the rare books in the Howlsley collection, unfailingly guided in his selections by the man who had given him access. With each passing day, he felt firmer in the conviction that Howlsley's work remained unfinished, and Santiago was the only one who could bring it to fruition.

So it came to pass that Santiago left grad school and devoted himself to the dark arts. Before encountering Howlsley, he had considered other career paths, such as law or consulting, but he was never able to feel enthusiastic about them. Witchcraft was another matter entirely. He could employ his considerable research training to filling in the gaps in Howlsley's library, and he actually found the art of spell craft satisfied his creative interests better than writing academic papers ever had. It was just a more rewarding career on a day-to-day basis—and the rewards if he pulled it off would be simply extraordinary... Admittedly, there were downsides as well. He had to tarnish his soul with several mortal sins before any spirits of significance would even come into contact with him. And the work could at times be exhausting. (It took him an embarrassing number of tries to get the resurrection trick to work properly.)

But ultimately, he was much happier after changing careers. The few people he saw thought he had gained a certain verve and confidence that they found very appealing. He had also found a new barber to make this newfound mojo manifest in his outer appearance, and now he thought he looked as awesome as he felt.

These building feelings of confidence were reinforced by his astounding progress in the ways of witchery. The hissing sound had never left him, and it seemed to guide him unerringly in his studies. It spoke to him with an immediacy that transcended language, and he learned not only to let the hissing guide him but also how to think like the Hisser, how to anticipate its directions. He had been chosen to act as the medium for an event that would reshape humanity, and thanks to the incredible diligence with which he had answered this calling it would not be long before the world trembled before the Highest One and marvel at the fantastic power of the Scholar.

The most difficult part of fulfilling the prophecy would be preparing the twelve priests. They had to be empty vessels who could channel the supreme will of the Scholar during the ceremony—in other words, they had to be dead and yet capable of chanting. This was a difficult task, one that could only be performed by finding business partners who could supplement Santiago's abilities with their own highly specialized set of skills. While was successful at reviving their bodies with his mastery of the dark arts, Santiago couldn't repair the psyches of his "priests" on his own, which meant he could only create clumsy servants incapable of higher functioning. Specifically, he needed them to have enough psychic coherence to be capable of performing the rituals of the sacrifice in a perfectly fluid manner. As this was not a problem that could be solved through the traditional dark arts, Santiago was forced to take out an online ad seeking technomages of extraordinary ability. Unfortunately, the majority of respondents proved disappointing—mostly cocksure young men who imagined themselves pros after taking an online course in neuromancy—and had to be dispatched with during their first encounter. The only two who didn't disappoint were Dana and Simon. The former was an absolute prodigy with both summoning spells and neural networks, while the latter was competent enough to keep up and had a much more malleable personality. Using a template programmed by Dana, Simon would implant each new recruit with a set of vague memories, habitual impulses, and a working base of knowledge about Bellwether University and Canaanite sacrificial rites. These memories and impulses didn't suffice to create a coherent new identity, but they provided the bare minimum amount of "personality" necessary to successfully accomplish assignments.

His reasons for culling the priests from the faculty were entirely practical: he needed people whose presence could be missed for a day or two without the majority of the campus noticing. The Lodge of the Owl had infiltrated enough of the College to keep a lot of things quiet, but even their network of spies would be helpless to quell the panic if students started to disappear en masse. (He calculated that he could successfully abduct students only for the shorter amount of time needed to prepare the sacrifice, and even so, his success would be assured only if there were a large enough distraction elsewhere on campus.) And it wouldn't do to target people with major functional roles in the day-to-day operations of the university—there would be too many points of contact where someone might notice what was wrong. No, the plan would depend on gathering faculty without any official administrative responsibilities. Only students would notice these people were gone, and it would take more than a week before they started raising an alarm about getting out of class. The choice to focus on contingent faculty in the *humanities* specifically was made solely on the principle of contiguity: As Santiago's focus was already on Howlsley Hall, his mind immediately turned to the departments who had offices there (English, Gender Studies, and Comp Lit).

In order to work the kinks out of this system, Santiago had his team try test runs at colleges all over the northern seaboard. It was a morbid activity but he had to be certain that he could trust his future priests for the ritual. At each site they used a different "procurer" to bring the faculty to their test site. Each procurer was an anonymous contract worker provided by the Lodge and would receive the code name "Ben Molche" for the duration of his service. In order to ensure anonymity, each "Ben Molche" would be killed after his allotted number of tasks were completed. It was during this period that Santiago came up with the idea of implanting the "priests" with memories of STEM instructors. The personality matrix was more or less arbitrary anyway, so there was no harm in making this adjustment, and the profiles of academics made the new recruits more comfortable on campus. Usually, he would just have these unfortunate scholars roam the libraries without end, since they seemed accustomed to this activity anyway. Of course, when he scaled up the operation at Bellwether, he couldn't have these reprogrammed former scholars roam their home institutions where they could easily be recognized. So the humanities faculty of Bellwether came to roam the halls of Wanesdale, futilely carrying around textbooks in subjects they didn't understand and viciously defensive of their new identities.

If the question were posed at the right moment, if he were somehow caught off guard at an especially depressive moment, Santiago might have admitted that his methods had become a little sloppy. There had been a breach of their facility, vague suspicions had been allowed to spread among some of the departmental administrators, his security team had been forced to add new staff after running short on properly vetted personnel... Really, his entire workforce had grown increasingly prone to mistakes as they rushed to have everything ready for the appointed date... And why exactly did everything have to happen on Friday, March 10? Only because he had boasted to the Lodge he could have it finished by that date. It was an arbitrary deadline, but the true Scholar should be able to meet any deadline he set for himself. It didn't matter if he was having trouble sleeping lately, if he was feeling increasingly on edge, or if he occasionally woke up in the middle of the night after dreaming that his knife wouldn't cut. To budge on the deadline would be tantamount to admitting that he was flawed. It would suggest that maybe he wasn't the Scholar anointed by history itself as the bringer of a new age. Santiago couldn't bear this implication, so he forged ahead with his arbitrary timeline.

And by the afternoon of March 10, everything was prepared. Santiago had successfully procured twelve priests and seven sacrifices, and they were all in position in Howlsley Hall. Now the ritual could begin.

CHAPTER TWENTY-EIGHT

Was it really worth it? Elena thought as they prepared her for the sacrifice. Was any of this really worth it at the end of the day? Sure, pursuing a PhD. had given her a chance to think deeply about issues that she cared about. And yes, she did really appreciate the opportunity to work closely with students, to watch their intellectual development firsthand, and to help them develop as scholars. She was incredibly proud to have played such a central role in the academic careers of wonderful, bright young people like Sasha. But was it really worth it for her? At a certain level, she just felt like academia demanded too much from her. She felt increasingly uncomfortable with how much of her life the job demanded—not only the time, but also the mental energy. There were no real breaks, no moments when she didn't feel a need to be "on." She never felt like she read or wrote anything for herself anymore. Even at night she would often lie awake thinking about teaching strategies or research, or agonizing over the general trajectory of her career. Like an overzealous floor manager with only one employee, she had learned to surveil herself at all times, constantly asking how every action contributed to her overall productivity. It was exhausting. Maybe at some point she had thought she could change academic culture from within—after she got tenure, maybe she would advocate for a total reconceptualization of academic work, a paradigm shift in academic culture...Who was she kidding? She didn't have a long-term plan other than holding on and hoping that it all proved to be worthwhile.

Such were Elena's thoughts as she was strapped onto a plank and laid out atop a giant pyre that Santiago and his crew had assembled in her Department's atrium. She was placed between Connie and poor Teddy Soplica, whose recent progress in Italian would evidently be in vain. A dozen figures in owl masks stood motionless around the border of the room. They were chanting in an unfamiliar language, while Simon and Dana walked up and down the rows, parodies of priests, sprinkling some kind of oil on the "offerings." Dana made a sign in the air. The Owls immediately stopped chanting and emitted a deafening low tone, which they held for two minutes before subsiding.

Of course, all the negativity didn't help, Elena reflected as one of the black-clad cultists (Simon, perhaps) tightened her straps. At a certain level, she had always felt that complaining about exploitation in the academic labor market was futile, whatever form it took: personal conversations, online think pieces, or even articles in professional publications. Any change was going to come in the form of concentrated pressure. (Incidentally, Elena regretted never being more involved in the unionization effort while she was in grad school, and she promised herself that she would learn more about the Bellwether faculty union if she managed to get out of this.) To the extent that people were already aware of problems in the higher ed labor market, dwelling on these issues just seemed like caressing a sore tooth. Elena couldn't stop doing it, and the more she did it, the less she wanted to stop. But she admitted it was counterproductive. All this commiseration didn't easily translate to collective action, and dwelling on her own suffering ultimately did more to paralyze Elena than anything else. And there was something else… Elena had been so caught up in understanding the academic job market and the situation of adjuncts in general that she kept losing sight of *herself* as an individual with a singular experience. Maybe part of deciding what one actually needed from an experience meant abstaining from any attempt to come to an objective evaluation—of the merits of the profession, the politics of the job market, or one's own abilities. Maybe she needed to stop asking if academia was worth it and ask instead: Was this profession giving her what she needed?

At this point, several Owls left the room and returned carrying torches. Santiago had now entered the room wearing a flowing black robe and his bull's head mask. His voice was surprisingly sonorous as he read a long incantation with refrains chanted by the Owls.

But then again, the issue wasn't really ever the adjunct crisis. Elena saw this very clearly as the torches began to lower toward the pyre. It was always a matter of control, recognition, desire, possession, bending, grabbing, pushing, breaking—in short, of love. Ultimately, Elena wanted to see herself through the eyes of the hiring committee, her students, her future colleagues, the tenure review board, her past professors, the jealous and underemployed members of her cohort (Connie included)… She wanted to delight in them seeing her as a Professor of Italian Literature—a mark of power and desirability that could only be conferred by the job market, a supreme arbiter, the magic of which was only confirmed by the seeming arbitrariness of its judgments. It was wrong to call what she was going through an adjunct crisis. No, it was a common crisis known to all lovers, losers, gamblers, entertainers—anyone who's ever needed their value confirmed against the odds. As it often happens, she had exaggerated the value of her beloved to incredible proportions, ever increasing this value as academia withheld reciprocation, and she had diminished herself in the process. What's more, she had reached a point where she wasn't sure she could go on like this. It wasn't that she had run out of desire, but she didn't think she could continue as the diminished self that the love now required. She didn't want to continue like this. It was just too great a sacrifice.

While Elena was reflecting upon all this, Connie had been working through a very different problem. During their failed escape attempt, she had managed to hang onto the knife that Ben had removed from his leg. When they were tied down this time it had slipped out of the waistband of her jeans, and so she had spent the greater part of Elena's internal monologue recovering it and discreetly getting to work at her own ropes. Once the torches had come out, she had decided not to worry so much about discretion and started awkwardly sawing at the rope with all her might. Just as the fires were lit, she broke free and rushed over to work on Elena's ropes (though her friend was evidently in shock and didn't notice her). Connie expected someone to rush in and try to stop her, but there was evidently some commotion among Santiago and the Owls. Connie couldn't figure out what was happening, but she could tell that several of them had fled from the room, and the pyre had only been lit at one end.

Even after the ropes came off, Elena still wasn't moving. Continuing to support her with one arm, Connie got to work on the ropes binding the next person over. Elena, still unresponsive, was getting heavy, and Connie didn't know how long she had until Santiago came back. So, she decided her main priority was to drag her friend out of the building.

"What about the others?" called out the young man Connie had just cut free.

"I have to get her out," Connie yelled. "I'll come back for them."

"Here—give me the knife," the young man yelled. "Just get her out of here."

Connie didn't have time to think. She handed the knife over and dragged Elena outside.

When they finally made it, the first face Connie encountered was a blustery old man, whose scowling lips and crinkled forehead looked oddly familiar. It was only much later in the evening that she successfully connected the unpleasant sensations she felt at the sight of this individual to the name Murray Otis. At the time Connie saw him, Otis was being protected by a row of security guards from an angry line of student protestors. Nearby, she spotted Santiago yelling about something while surrounded by several Owls and security guards. She didn't have time to figure out what they were talking about, as a young woman ran out of the building moments later and soundlessly grabbed at Connie, evidently trying to ask for help. Thinking quickly, Connie hurried this woman and Elena into the throng of protestors so that Santiago wouldn't see them. As soon as she reached the crowd of protestors, Connie had to hang back herself as Santiago and his Owls were already marching back toward the entrance.

"How many got out?" Santiago asked, meeting Simon and Dana by the door.

"Three," Simon responded. "Luckily we have plenty of priests. We can just close three of them in the building and call it a night."

"No," Santiago said in an irritated voice. "Sadly, we cannot do that. The Owls are already dead—their souls can no longer be offered. We need *living* sacrifices." At this moment, Simon suddenly felt himself unable to move. Dana, who had been trying to sneak away quietly along the side of the building, fell over a few yards away. Two security guards carried her back over to Santiago. "This will be where we part ways. It's unfortunate, but our leadership is undergoing a bit of restructuring, and there's just no use for your current positions anymore."

Santiago made a gesture, and the same two security guards dragged Simon and Dana into the building. Next, he noticed Murray Otis still standing nearby, angry and confused. "Mr. Otis," he called out jovially. "It is an honor to finally meet you," Santiago said, taking the older man under his arm. "You must be wondering what the hold up is for your lecture. And I'm sure all of this looks quite strange. I assure that it's merely a college tradition, sort of like a pep rally—hence, so many people dressed up like our mascot. We meant to have everything finished earlier, but we're running a little behind schedule. Let me show you to your lecture hall…"

* * *

Teddy Soplica didn't know the woman who had cut him free and was now dragging his unconscious Italian professor out the door. More generally, he didn't understand anything happening around him. He only knew that he very much wanted to run. But Professor Malatesta obviously needed help right now, and someone had to stay behind to get the others out. So Teddy made a split second decision to tell this woman that he would stay behind and free the others. But even as he was taking the knife from her hand, he started to regret his reflexive heroism. It was as if feeling the weight of the knife suddenly reminded him that this was all very real—and dangerous. But the decision had been made, and now freeing the others was something he had to do.

Teddy immediately got to work on freeing the nearest person to him, a young woman he vaguely recognized from the dining hall. After only a few moments of sawing at the ropes, she was free to run away and running toward the door. Teddy felt relieved. At this rate, he would be able to have everyone cut free in no time, and they could all escape before the fires spread.

He ran over to the next stake in the row and was surprised to recognize this person—it was a kid from his dorm whom he had often seen in the common room. This time things didn't go so smoothly. Right at the moment when he brought the knife into contact with the rope, Teddy heard a deafening screech close by and felt a searing pain in his right arm. Looking down, he saw a scrunched-up white face flanked by enormous wings. The creature dug further into his arm and caused him to drop the knife. When he bent over to pick it up, it leapt from his arm crashed into the back of his head, knocking him over.

Splayed on the floor, Teddy found his limbs completely paralyzed by an unknown force. He watched helplessly as three more people were shoved on top of the pyre and the returning masked figures finished setting the fires.

A look of resignation on Rogelio's face was the last thing Teddy saw.

CHAPTER TWENTY-NINE

When Elena regained her senses, she was lying on the grass outside Howlsley Hall. The building was ablaze, and a crowd of stunned students holding protest signs stood all around her. Connie was sitting next to her, silently watching the fire. Elena slowly sat up and saw her old film student Solange walking away from the fire in a daze. "Did we all make it?" Elena asked.

"I don't know," Connie didn't look at Elena as she answered. "Probably not all of us."

"Did they…um…you know…?"

Connie shrugged. "There's no giant hell spawn lording over us yet."

"Let's call it a win, then?" Elena said.

But she didn't feel like they had won. Connie was preoccupied with something, and there was an eerie silence around her, an improper silence, as if there were a hole in the aural landscape. "Where's the fire department?" Elena finally asked.

Connie didn't respond. Sitting there, Elena realized that there was something else wrong: no one was on their phones calling for help. Why? With a vague fear, she turned around and saw what looked like a hazy green wall rising up near the highway and arcing over the campus, closing it off at each end. It was almost as if some kind of magical bubble had blocked Bellwether off from the rest of the world.

At that moment, two beings emerged from the burning building. One was gaunt, and the other powerfully built. As they walked away from the flames, Elena could see that the larger figure was a woman in old-fashioned dress with a round face and dark, close-set eyes. But it was the gaunt figure that arrested her attention. On closer examination, it was actually a walking

128

skeleton, its exposed bones standing against the bright flames as a terrible silhouette. The woman made a sign and the skeleton began to give off a green glow and slowly regain organs and flesh. Even before his face was fully restored, Elena could recognize this figure from his imperious bearing, as she had seen his portrait in the library so many times. As she recoiled in horror at this recognition, she heard a loud cry and saw something tear through his still forming chest cavity.

"Connie!" Elena shouted out. Connie had grabbed one of the protestors' signs and was jamming the wooden stake into the skeleton's chest. The wood tore easily through the still-forming flesh, and Connie kept stabbing until the skeleton fell over motionless. Elena watched in horror as the woman next to him, with a shriek, suddenly distorted her face into a hideous birdlike visage and grew talons on her fingers. Before this woman could touch Connie, however, Elena saw a man in black and another young woman rushed up and knocked this frightful apparition to the ground. After a brief struggle, Connie and her two new companions had succeeded in subduing the woman with the claws.—"Sasha?!" Elena called out, suddenly recognizing the young woman who had come to help.— Working together, Connie, Sasha, and the man in black lifted up the terrifying bird woman and threw her into the flames. There was a momentary green flash, followed by an eerie period of silence during which all the flames appeared to stand still. Then, they heard a terrible scream and saw the building devoured, the green bubble overhead soundlessly dispersing into the night sky.

* * *

A little later in the evening, Sasha, Connie, and Elena were sitting on the steps outside Connie's apartment. It was a nice night, much warmer than anyone would have expected earlier in the week. When police and fire finally arrived at Bellwether campus, they had decided to get away before they had to answer any questions. (Foremost among the many things they didn't think they could explain, Connie was afraid the police wouldn't believe that the skinless body lying in front of Howlsley was already a skeleton before she stabbed it.) After being confined indoors all day, Connie and Elena had both insisted on sitting outside.

Sasha explained to them what had interrupted the ritual.

It was ultimately a fortunate accident that had allowed them to escape. After all, Sasha had known only that the Murray Otis lecture had been planned to divert attention from something, and she had correctly inferred that this something was happening in Howlsley. So her plan was simple. If someone didn't want anyone near Howlsley Hall, she would bring the student protestors there. She had diverted Murray Otis to Howlsley for this reason, instructing Nate—*"Who?"* "The guy who helped me and Connie beat up the claw lady. He was like a rogue security guard or something" *"Ah."*—to spread the word among the hired security that the lecture had been moved, while also sending texts to the student organizers she had met while researching her article. The idea was that this news would lead everyone to converge on Howlsley Hall. And it did! But the circumstance that freed Connie and Elena was only incidentally a result of Sasha's preparations.

Entering Howlsley Hall with Otis, Sasha stopped in the entrance to respond to texts from the organizers she had contacted. Otis had gone ahead, and Sasha could only guess what went through his mind next. This man had written on many occasions about the university as a literal site of indoctrination into paganism, and to his credit his subsequent actions proved him to be sincere in these beliefs. Although Sasha had only seen vaguely what was going on, based on Elena's and Connie's recollections, Otis must have seen a man in a bull-head mask surrounded by mysterious owl people carrying torches, preparing to light a pyre on which lay several bound students. Upon encountering this horrific sight, Otis let out a guttural cry—"Soros!"—and tackled the bull man from behind. This action threw the bull man off balance and must have caused some panic among the people dressed as owls, as they quickly started to crowd around their assaulted comrade. Then, security rushed in and dragged Otis, Sasha, and the bull-headed guy from the building, trailed by all the owl folk. There seemed to be some disagreement among the security guards as to who was at fault—some attempted to detain Otis and others restrained the bullheaded man. It must have been while Santiago was arguing with security that Connie and Elena escaped.

"So" Elena asked after a pause, "what do you think happened to Santiago?" With a sudden chill, she recalled the image of him appearing in Connie's parking lot the night before. Should they really be sitting out here celebrating? After all, he still knew where Connie lived… What would they do if he came back for revenge?

* * *

Santiago didn't like to admit when he made mistakes. But as he stood outside the sacrificial furnace that had previously been Howlsley Hall, it was getting harder and harder to deny that something had gone seriously wrong with his plan. The last straw was when he saw that Asian woman he had tried to sacrifice stabbing to second death the resurrected David Howlsley and teaming up with what were apparently two random passersby to return Anna Sowa to the hell dimension. At this point, he felt fairly certain that something had gone wrong. Maybe suddenly switching gears to make "Ben

Molche" one of his priests this morning wasn't the greatest idea—after all, he hadn't vetted him for his aptitude in foreign languages. (Christ, Santiago had barely talked to him; for all he knew, "Ben" had a serious speech impediment that persisted after his "reassignment.") Or maybe the incantation was more time sensitive than he had thought; maybe they shouldn't have just kept going after that old crackpot interrupted the "Chant of the Beckoning Chasm." Or maybe Santiago should have just worn the traditional headdress instead of the custom-designed bull mask he had added to the ceremony for dramatic flare—he had convinced himself that the Voice wanted him to wear it, but maybe he was just having auditory hallucinations from a lack of sleep... While he didn't know exactly where things had gone wrong, he was absolutely certain that the fire engulfing the building was supposed to be magenta, instead of, well, flame-colored with flashes of green. Instead of a new era, the certainty slowly dawned on him that he didn't actually succeed in physically manifesting the Highest One on this mortal plane.

Of course, if he were to look at the positive, he could say that the momentary appearance of Howlsley and Sowa among the living at least confirmed that he had successfully opened some kind of portal—and to the correct dimension at that. For most aspiring young dabblers in the dark arts, this would be a remarkable feat, but it was cold comfort now. There was just no prize for almost succeeding in manifesting an ancient being. No, when everything was said and done, this whole thing was a failure: as it turned out, this arcane ritual act of human sacrifice was not going to give Santiago the validation he had so badly wanted. Part of him couldn't help wondering if maybe he should have stayed in grad school after all...

Anyway, there was no sense in continuing to stand by the gateway in the vain hope of greeting his ascendant dark lord. Despite his disappointment, Santiago still had the sense to realize it was time to make a speedy getaway. But the moment he tried to run, Santiago felt an iron grip holding him back. There was someone digging into his ankle hard, and as much as he struggled, he couldn't wrench himself free. He felt an enormous weight pulling him toward the fiery wreckage of Howlsley Hall. Falling to the ground, he clawed at the pavement in a vain attempt to slow his descent. Turning around, he saw a horrific, yet strangely familiar, mass of iron and burned flesh staring back at him from the flames. His leg was in the unrelenting grip of this thing's giant metallic arm. "Please, no," he called out pitifully as his body steadily approached the flames.

Dana didn't say anything in response. She simply curled her steel mouth into a smile and dragged Santiago down to Hell.

CHAPTER THIRTY

Although the events at Bellwether College were reported as a national tragedy, the details never became widely known. Investigators managed to identify one survivor of the conflagration, a female student who had run out of the building shortly before the first reports of smoke, but she was evidently too traumatized to give a cogent narrative of what happened. A search was made for the overzealous private security forces who, according to the student protestors at the scene, had used excessive force to hold them back from the Howlsley building. Not only did this search turn up nothing, but several senior members of campus security apparently vanished into thin air before the police could question them. Most alarmingly, at least seventeen people were missing after the fire: four students, twelve faculty members, and Murray Otis. Several people had seen Otis enter the building with two unidentified individuals immediately before the fire, and the one surviving student claimed there were other students still inside when she got away. On the basis of these reports, the students and Otis were feared dead. (It was less clear what happened to the missing faculty—there were reports of other people in the vicinity of the building, but these reports were too confused to ascertain who these individuals were.) Strangely, however, the only human remains found at the site of the fire were identified as being roughly one hundred years old. Try as they might, no one could tease a coherent narrative from the evidence, and the press naturally assumed that the fire must have somehow been related to the campus protests. Headlines included "Liberal Snowflakes Go On Violent Rampage," "Firebrand Otis Ignites Bellwether Campus [Video]," "Student Organizers Blame Anarchist Agitators," "Ten Things You Need to Know About the Recent Campus Fires," and "What the Internet Isn't Saying About the Bellwether Incident." Conjectures of possible cult influence on these events were confined to fringe websites and buried threads on online message boards, and here they appeared only in distorted form: the most widespread version claimed that the cultic rites leading to the fire were part of a scheme hatched at Bohemian Grove and funded by George Soros, possibly with the collusion of the Clinton Foundation, to create sacrificial shrines in Planned Parenthood facilities across the nation. There was one paranormal expert who had the presence of mind to conjecture, during an interview on an Australian podcast on unexplained phenomena, that the missing victims and unusual burn patterns at the site of the fire may be evidence that an inter-dimensional portal was opened briefly on the site of Howlsley Hall through the (mostly unsuccessful) performance of an ancient sacrificial rite—but even the podcast's hosts poked fun at this "baseless speculation."

Elena didn't know what became of Santiago, or who else may have been involved in his scheme. But it didn't matter. The websites for Moahil Loch and International Horizons were no longer active, she had got the lock on her door fixed, no more uninvited guests showed up at her home or office—her involvement in the matter appeared to be over.

The thing that kept bothering Elena was Teddy. After she had recovered from her initial shock, Elena remembered that she had seen Solange standing in the crowd alongside Connie right after they had escaped. When Elena asked Connie how Solange had got free, she was reluctant to answer at first, but then she told her that a lanky blond boy had insisted on taking the knife when Connie was dragging Elena out. He must have cut Solange free. Also… He hadn't come out.

Elena immediately understood that Connie was talking about Teddy. It was an extraordinary thing to realize—one of her students saving another. Of all the implausible things that had happened, this was the one that stuck with her. It was impossible to believe that the somewhat shy young man who always paired off with "Mario" to write zany in-class dialogues was secretly a hero, or even just a potential hero, all along. How could it be that another of her former students was alive because of him?

So when the Soplicas finally accepted the probable and held a memorial for Teddy, Elena attended. She had met his family only once, when they took a tour of campus while picking him up the previous spring. At the time, she had lied and told them that he was an especially gifted student and making strong progress in the course. This year she could have told them honestly that he had really impressed her and become one of the top students in the class… Now, she wanted them to know that he wasn't just a good kid or a promising student—he was a hero. But she also couldn't tell the whole story. It would be too hard to believe many of the details, and more importantly, she didn't want them to picture Teddy tied to the stake, watching a mad cult make the preparations for his death. Instead, she told them this:

"Excuse me, Mr. and Mrs. Soplica. I just wanted to let you know that I was there that night. I saw your son go into the building after the fire started and pull a young girl from the building. Then, he went in again to save someone else—and he didn't come back. I'm not sure how many other people saw this, but just in case no one had told you, I wanted to let you know. Your son is a hero."

This was a good lie, Elena thought. It cut away all the unnecessary details and reduced the story to what needed to be remembered. She wished her own memory worked that way; she hoped it would one day. In the meantime, she would keep telling Teddy's story to more and more people.

* * *

Would Elena miss academia? She thought about the question a lot now. Frankly, after the physical disappearance of her department from campus, she didn't see much chance of the College renewing the Italian program. In fact, there were already rumors that they were planning to build a new business school on the site of Howlsley Hall, including talk of naming it after a(n in)famous(ly segregationist) governor who had gone to Bellwether. It was still spring, so there would be plenty of part-time and short-term academic jobs posted in the coming months, but somehow Elena didn't feel especially motivated to apply. Was it too late to apply to law school? Was that guy she knew at Lippman Publishing still looking for copyeditors? If surviving a ritual sacrifice at the hands of a demented cult had given her anything, it was the feeling that she could leave academia on her own terms. She had more or less literally survived the fiery wreckage of her cherished dreams and now could march confidently forth—to learn how people actually went about applying to jobs in other fields.

(Incidentally, Elena sometimes wished there was a more heroic cultural mythology surrounding the vicissitudes of gainful employment. Although one's emotional life could become so deeply entwined with a career, it was difficult to describe disappointment on this front with an uplifting sense of pathos. Discussions devolved too easily into self-pity or toothless irony, rendering major career disappointments as overblown personal failings or no big deal.)

Yes, she would certainly miss academic life. In the daytime, the campus could be such a soothing place, especially in the short period between the deadline for spring grades and graduation, when the weather was warm and the campus felt nearly empty, except for a handful of seniors lounging here and there. Elena didn't think she could ever grow tired of the stately buildings and manicured lawns. Admittedly, this was partly for aesthetic reasons—the facades of a well-kept campus radiated a sensation of wealth and luxury that afforded her seemingly endless pleasure and comfort—but it was also because she would always believe in what they stood for. Not even an absurd, stupidly violent cult could make her doubt the basic mission of higher education. She believed it was absolutely essential for young adults to learn how to ask intelligent and critical questions about themselves and their world; she thought the microcosm of the campus was an ideal way for them to learn about their abilities and obligations within a larger community; she had endless respect for the ritual of students dedicating themselves in successive generations to honest, probing thought. Elena was sad to leave this environment even after everything she had gone through at Bellwether.

But she also knew she was done with it—in a certain sense at least. She couldn't keep engaging with the university in the way she had been doing. For all this time, she had been caught up on the question of why she wasn't succeeding, why her career never seemed match the ideal trajectory she had so carefully planned, but she hadn't seriously questioned whether the career she had imagined was a good thing *for her*. She had been caught up in a vicious cycle of self-interrogation over the ways in which she seemed to be falling short of the University's demands, but she had thought comparatively little about her own demands. What did *she* need to have a fulfilling career and a satisfying professional life? And if she were honest, academia hadn't been all that fulfilling for a while now. Instead, she was mostly motivated by fear—of falling behind, of bad student evaluations, of low enrollments, of not making it.

Now, she was surprised to notice that she woke up a few weeks after the fire with a tremendous sense of relief. Her fears had been realized in a more grotesque fashion than she could have imagined—and she had survived. Moreover, there were just so many things that she didn't have to care about now. New trends in the field, the politics at X journal, how she felt about the digital humanities… None of it was her concern anymore. And the fact that she didn't have to discuss ideas with people professionally made her feel all the more eager to do so. It was as if a large portion of her mental life had been returned to her possession. She actually cared about her research more now that she didn't have to come up with a two-minute description for anyone… And of course, this feeling also raised a great amount of uncertainty for her. Would she keep writing about Mario Bava now that there was no strong career incentive to do so? Did she want to write something for a more general audience—maybe an essay on why horror fans should consider the giallo genre as more than just a guilty pleasure? Or maybe she needed to train herself off of the vestigial need to produce some kind of writing to commemorate every turn in her mental life?

In short, it was a deeply ambivalent moment. While she had a certain, possibly unconsciously romanticized, feeling of freedom and rediscovered curiosity, Elena also wanted to find a way to relate to the past nine years of her life so that they didn't feel like a waste. The loss and sense of possibility were both tremendous, and she didn't really know whether she was happy that her life as an adjunct was over. For now, she simply wanted to explore things that she never seemed to have time for before. Maybe she would finally learn to cook or read some Russian literature. The thought that she could decide what to do next without worrying about how it reflected on her status as a potentially promising young scholar was exhilarating. For the moment at least, she felt happy, energetic, and ready to leave academia behind, possibly forever.

* * *

"Wait, so you've just been sitting around reading Chekhov?" Connie asked after listening to Elena explain at length how perfectly "The Black Monk" illuminates the relationship between megalomania and academic ambition.

"He's sooo good!" Elena responded. "But I've been doing other stuff too. Actually, I wanted to read you this. This is an actual excerpt from that Pietro guy's book:

"*It's better to live one day as a lion than 100 years as a sheep.* How does this adage apply to today's business environment? You must always be on the advance, charging forward and carrying your team along with you. Never be satisfied with merely performing the requirements of your position and going home to watch TV. There's always something more you can be doing. If you dedicate yourself fully to every task, your enthusiasm will be infectious, and it will inspire your employees to lay it all on the line for the company's benefit. Remember that good management is the marriage of the corporation and the self.'

"It goes on like this... I would feel guilty if I thought anyone would ever actually read it."

"At least, it's better than my cover letters," Connie said, masterfully turning the conversation back to herself. "I'm actually still a little pissed that I can't list staking a zombie and defeating a shapeshifter as a transitional moment in my identity as a scholar. I mean, it kinda was."

"You can always try it," Elena shrugged. "Just remember you only get two pages max, ideally less. If you want to explain the whole cult thing, you're going to have to seriously shorten your dissertation synopsis."

"Why is this so hard?" Connie pushed her laptop away and took a sip of coffee. She liked that the little pterodactyl on her coffee cup seemed so carefree. "By the way, you probably don't want to talk about Bellwether, but I was wondering about that Sasha girl. Are they going to let her finish the Italian major?"

"Actually, yeah. She's taking the fall semester off—a lot of students are doing that, for some reason—and studying abroad in the spring. You know, with a real program. So, that will give her enough credits for the major. Or at least close enough. Victor's a good guy—he promised to make sure the Registrar counts the credits generously in light of the... complications on the Department's end."

Connie pulled her laptop toward her again, typed a couple lines, and then deleted them.

"What's the best way to put, 'I'd be eager to teach anything you need covered, but I also have hyper-specific interests that perfectly match your department's needs?'"

"Want me to ask Pietro?"

Connie tried to type a little more, only to push her laptop away again. "Maybe I should quit too."

Elena shrugged. "Give it another year."

Made in the USA
Columbia, SC
20 March 2020